"Why Are You Walking Me Out?" She Asked.

"So every man in the place knows that you are with me."

"Am I with you, Steven?"

"Yes, you are."

"Just for tonight?"

"No. I want to have you by my side again."

They stepped out into the March evening. It was damp and chilly and Ainsley shivered. If they'd had a different relationship he would have wrapped his arm around her. But then he thought the hell with that. He put his arm over her shoulder and drew her against the curve of his body.

She shuddered and looked up at him.

In her eyes he read the same desire he'd been battling all night. He saw that she was thinking of him as a man—not a colleague. And he knew that he'd do anything to keep that interest alive.

Dear Reader,

Steven Devonshire is the next illegitimate son of Malcolm Devonshire we meet in this story. He has always lived by his own rules. His mother is a Nobel Prize–winning physicist who is working on the God particle and never really had much time for anyone outside her laboratory.

Steven is very much her son. He is driven and determined to prove to the world that he is just as talented and can be more successful than both his mother and his father.

Ainsley is just as determined as Steven to prove to the world that she is more than she used to be. Steven ignored her once before, but Ainsley scarcely resembles the woman she used to be. In fact, as a powerful and very sexy magazine editor in chief, she has caught Steven's attention.

Steven isn't used to anyone else calling the shots, and he soon finds himself battling for control with Ainsley in a relationship neither is sure they want to commit to—even though their bodies and their hearts say otherwise!

I hope you enjoy *Scandalizing the CEO!*

Happy reading,

Katherine

KATHERINE GARBERA

SCANDALIZING THE CEO

Silhouette®

Desire

Published by Silhouette Books
America's Publisher of Contemporary Romance

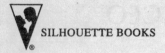

SILHOUETTE BOOKS

ISBN-13: 978-0-373-73020-9

SCANDALIZING THE CEO

Recycling programs
for this product may
not exist in your area.

Recent Books by Katherine Garbera

Silhouette Desire

†*His Wedding-Night Wager* #1708
†*Her High-Stakes Affair* #1714
†*Their Million-Dollar Night* #1720
The Once-A-Mistress Wife #1749
****Make-Believe Mistress* #1798
****Six-Month Mistress* #1802
****High-Society Mistress* #1808
**The Greek Tycoon's Secret Heir* #1845
**The Wealthy Frenchman's Proposition* #1851
**The Spanish Aristocrat's Woman* #1858
Baby Business #1888
§*The Moretti Heir* #1927
§*The Moretti Seduction* #1935
§*The Moretti Arrangement* #1943
Taming the Texas Tycoon #1952
‡*Master of Fortune* #1999
‡*Scandalizing the CEO* #2007

†What Happens in Vegas…
**The Mistresses
*Sons of Privilege
§Moretti's Legacy
‡The Devonshire Heirs

KATHERINE GARBERA

is a strong believer in happily-ever-after. She's written more than thirty-five books and has been nominated for career achievement awards in series fantasy and series adventure from *RT Book Reviews*. Her books have appeared on the Waldenbooks/Borders bestseller list for series romance and on the *USA TODAY* extended bestseller list. Visit Katherine on the Web at www.katherinegarbera.com.

Printed in U.S.A.

For all my readers.

Prologue

Steven Devonshire ignored the first two summonses from his biological father, but when his mother had called and had asked him to please attend a meeting at the Everest Group in downtown London, he relented.

Stepping into the boardroom and finding his two half brothers there was unexpected as well. His half brothers and he were referred to collectively as the "Devonshire heirs" in some circles and the "Devonshire bastards" in others. They had all been born in the same year to three different mothers.

Malcolm Devonshire freely admitted to being their father and had done his duty as far as contributing financially to their upbringing. Steven had no idea what relationship Henry and Geoff had with Malcolm, but Steven had never met the man before.

Henry, the middle brother and the son of Tiffany

Malone, seventies pop star, had grown up to be a famous rugby player. After an injury a couple of years ago, he'd given up playing and taken up doing more endorsement deals and starring in a couple of reality television shows, from what Steven had heard in the gossip rags.

"Malcolm has prepared a message for you," Edmond said. Edmond was Malcolm's solicitor. Steven had met Edmond many times and actually found the older man to be good company.

The Everest Group had always been Malcolm Devonshire's life. It didn't surprise Steven that the one time he'd thought he'd meet his father, the location was this office. Malcolm had just turned seventy and probably wanted to make sure that his life's work didn't end with his own death.

Geoff was the eldest of the three of them and the son of Princess Louisa of Strathearn, a minor royal. He and Steven had almost met before—they were both supposed to attend Eton College but Geoff never matriculated.

"Mr. Devonshire is dying," Edmond said. "He wants the legacy he worked so hard to create to live on in each of you."

"He didn't create that empire for us," Steven said. Malcolm did things for himself—not for anyone else. Malcolm had never done anything that didn't benefit the Everest Group. Steven suspected that Malcolm must want something from them now. But what?

"If you would all please sit down and allow me to explain…" Edmond said.

Steven sat down, as did the two other men. By nature he was someone who was used to having things go his way. He knew how to turn every new opportunity to his advantage and saw no reason why he wouldn't be able to do that with whatever Malcolm had in mind.

As Edmond spoke, it became apparent that Malcolm wanted them to take over his businesses. Whichever one of them was most successful—financially—would be given the chairmanship of the entire conglomerate.

Steven tried to digest everything. He didn't care about the sappy emotionality of an offer from his dying father, but he was interested in the business angle. He owned a very successful, high-end china company.

And if he won the competition with his half brothers that would be the icing on the cake. He relished the thought of winning and knew he would. He wasn't like Henry—too used to the spotlight—or like Geoff—too used to the pampered, privileged life of a royal. Steven realized he was exactly the right person to win this.

Edmond nodded to the three of them and left the room. As soon as the door closed behind Edmond, Steven stood up.

"I think we should do it," Steven said. He doubted that the deal would stand if they all weren't in on it. Whatever Malcolm's ulterior motive, Steven knew they all had to be involved.

Fortunately, each of the men agreed as well. As they all stood around the boardroom table, Steven listened to his half brothers chat. The men were strangers to him, but he was used to going it alone. He'd never been a team player, to which Steven attributed his own success. He knew what needed to be done and did it. Himself.

Henry stepped out to find Edmond so they could inform him of their decision. After the other men left, Steven lingered. He wanted to know what Malcolm's motivation was in all this.

"Why now?" he asked. Edmond's mentorship to Steven gave him an opening, and he had never hesitated to use whatever resources he had to get by in business and in life.

"As I explained, Mr. Devonshire's failing health is motivating him…" Edmond began, but Steven cut him off.

"To worry about the company he gave his life to," Steven concluded. He knew enough about the absentee father to understand what he was thinking. It was exactly what Steven had expected. The Everest Group was Malcolm Devonshire's life and now that his life was ending, the last thing he wanted was to see the company fail. Other men might try to pass on something to their offspring, but Malcolm wanted the company he'd created and nurtured to thrive long after he was gone.

"Indeed," Edmond agreed.

Steven didn't need the confirmation from Edmond. He had already figured it out himself. Malcolm had always been easy for Steven to understand because he saw a lot of his father's public traits in himself. He was able to focus on a task at hand and set aside the emotionality that often derailed others. He knew how to make sacrifices in order to achieve the results he desired.

"I'm not sure that I want a part of this," Steven noted. "This competition isn't fair. The other men don't have the experience I have in business. They can't compete with me."

"I think you'll find they have their own strengths," Edmond said.

He didn't like Edmond's inference that there were strengths to the other men that he couldn't perceive. Steven prided himself on being able to read anyone.

He would meet with them later—get to know them so he'd make sure he won. Winning wasn't something that Steven was willing to let slide.

"I'll be checking in with you over the next few months to make sure you stay on track," Edmond said.

Steven shook his head. He hated having someone looking over his shoulder and he didn't need it. "I'll send you an e-mail once a week with our numbers and updating you on my action agenda for increasing our revenue."

"I'm also available, as ever, to offer my advice should you need it. I've been at Malcolm's side since the first day he started his company."

"I guess that makes you the longest relationship of his life," Steven said.

"Too true. Business is at the heart of it…and I think we are both comfortable with that."

Steven nodded. The emotionality thing again. The key to success was to stay distanced from others. Men started making stupid decisions when they thought they had something to lose.

"Save your advice for the other men," Steven said. "I prefer to work alone."

The older man narrowed his eyes, but Steven gave him no chance to argue. He didn't answer to his father's second in command.

"Have a good day, Edmond."

Steven walked out of the boardroom and out of the office building. The Everest Mega Store, in his hands, would become the premiere shopping destination for pop culture.

When people talked about the Devonshire bastards, they

wouldn't remember just the star rugby player or the son of a royal. No, they would remember Steven and the fact that he was the best.

One

"I've got an idea," Steven said to Dinah as soon as his executive vice president at Raleighvale China answered the phone.

"The last time you said that I found myself answering some rather uncomfortable questions from the police in Rome."

He laughed. "This time you won't have to deal with the police."

"Somehow my fears still aren't eased. What's this idea of yours?"

"What do you know about pop culture?"

"Why?"

"How does a position as my executive VP sound?"

"I thought that *was* my position," she said.

"For Everest Group Mega Store. I'm calling you from my new office."

."Your father's company? You said you'd never do that. Why now?"

Steven didn't talk about his personal life. *Ever.*

"My reasons are my own. Suffice it to say that there is a huge bonus in it for you if you help me make this company the top performer at Everest Group."

"Very well. When do you need me?" Dinah asked.

"In twenty-four hours or so. I need time to acclimate and find an office for you. Bring your admin for now, but once you're settled, we'll find someone else to work in the other office."

"Twenty-four hours is pretty quick," she said.

"I'll be in touch," he said.

"Steven?"

"Yes?"

"Are you sure about this? I know you—"

"I always am," he said, hanging up the phone. No one really knew him and certainly not Dinah. She only knew the part of him he allowed her to see.

Steven had taken the china company over from his grandfather. Founded in 1780 to compete with Wedgwood, Raleighvale had succeeded in creating a truly English style of tableware. They were now the royal china makers, something that Dinah Miller spent a lot of time touting to prospective clients. She recently secured for them a bid to make Raleighvale the official dinnerware for the new president of France. He knew she'd be equally successful in her new role.

His iPhone beeped, notifying him of an incoming text message. It was from Geoff, requesting that he meet him and Henry for a drink at the Athenaeum Club. He replied in the affirmative.

Then his phone rang. "Devonshire."

"This is Hammond from the Leicester Square store. I'm sorry to bother you, sir, but we have an emergency."

"Why isn't the duty manager handling this?" Steven asked. He didn't remember seeing Hammond's name on the list of managers at that location.

"I'm a retail floor specialist. The manager isn't here, she's on her lunch break and won't answer her phone. But we can't wait until she gets back."

"What is the situation?" Steven asked.

"Someone has set up and is doing a photo shoot in the middle of the selling floor. It's Jon BonGiovanni, the rocker, and there is a crowd of people blocking the elevator. They just won't move."

"I'll be right there."

He hung up and grabbed his suit jacket before leaving to take care of the problem at the Leicester Square store. He didn't have time for waffling—the last thing he needed on his first day was some sort of retail fiasco.

Upon reaching the Leicester Square store, he took two steps and stopped, gobsmacked.

The problem with the store was obvious. A model, photographer and photographer's assistant milled about in the main retail section—just as Hammond had said. It was only as he walked closer that he saw Jon BonGiovanni, the aging rock musician from the seventies supergroup Majestica standing under the photographer's lights.

He wore a pair of skintight jeans and a barely there American flag shirt displaying his bare chest with a tattoo of a fist in the center of it.

"What's going on here?" Steven said as he approached the group.

"We are trying to do a photo shoot. One that your CEO

has already approved, but today no one seems to know what was agreed on," the photographer said.

"I'm the CEO. Steven Devonshire."

"I'm Davis Montgomery."

Steven had heard of Davis—who hadn't? The man had made a mint photographing young rockers like Bob Dylan, John Lennon, Mick Jagger and Janis Joplin in the early seventies. His open approach to photography and his subjects had changed the way rock portraits were taken and revolutionized photography.

Steven shook the man's hand. "It's a pleasure to meet you. But you can't shoot in the retail store during our busy selling time."

"Ainsley received permission for us to be here."

"Who is Ainsley?"

"I am."

The woman who walked up behind him was...exquisite. She had thick, ebony-colored hair that hung from a high ponytail at the back of her head. Her dark hair and alabaster skin first captured his attention but as his gaze skimmed down her body, he was entranced by her feminine figure. Her blouse was slim-fitting with cap sleeves and a nipped-in waist, and then the curvy hips were hugged lovingly by the black skirt. She was his dream girl come to life. The thick red belt around her waist just accentuated her gorgeous figure.

And then he caught a glimpse of her legs and the silk hose that encased them.

He nearly groaned out loud. She was a Betty Page look-alike. That classic fifties pin-up girl who had captured his teenage imagination and never let it go.

"And who are you, Ms. Ainsley?"

She seemed a bit taken aback by the question, and he

wondered if he should have known who she was without asking. But she had a distinctively American accent and she was clearly in either the fashion industry or music. But he knew he would have remembered her had they met.

"Ainsley Patterson, editor-in-chief of *British Fashion Quarterly.*"

"Your name is familiar, but I don't believe we've had the pleasure of meeting before."

"That's great," Davis said. "Now you know each other and I'd like to get back to work."

"I'm sure that Mr. Devonshire will be more than happy to accommodate us. After all, we have the permission of his father's solicitor."

Steven was tired of hearing about his father. Malcolm and he were little more than strangers. Though the same could be said of his mother and him. He just had never been the kind of child who'd clung to his parents.

"That's all well and good, Ms. Patterson, but neither Malcolm nor his lawyer are here right now. Let's go up to my office and discuss what you need and find a time that will work for everyone."

Steven expected Ainsley to back down, but she didn't. He'd never met a woman who could be so sexy and so businesslike at the same time. It was a turn-on just talking to her, but somehow he knew that wasn't the route he should take.

Ainsley didn't want to spend any extra time speaking to a man who couldn't remember her. But she hadn't gotten to where she was in publishing by avoiding people who annoyed her. Davis gave her a look that said he was about to blow his top and they were going to have to deal with one of his infamous temper tantrums.

"Come on. I don't have all day to hang out here," Jon said.

"Jon, I'm sorry for this inconvenience. Why don't you take a ten-minute break and Mr. Devonshire and I will straighten this out."

"Will we?" Steven said.

He had a look that was straight out of a fashion magazine: short hair, styled to look as if he didn't care, blue eyes—Paul Newman blue. So bright and penetrating Ainsley had been mesmerized by him the first time they'd met.

Of course, back then she'd been seventy pounds heavier, five years younger and minus the self-confidence she had today.

"Yes, we will. I'm sure that there is something we can offer you that will be adequate compensation—though having your store featured in our magazine is quite a boon."

"From your perspective, perhaps," Steven said.

"What can we do to make this happen?" she asked.

"I'm thinking feature articles on the Devonshire heirs," Steven said.

"That would be interesting, but we are a women's fashion magazine," she said. Her mind going over what she knew about Steven and his half brothers. The real angle would be getting them to talk about their early years, but even then there wasn't a fashion twist. Maybe the mothers, she thought. Then she knew she had it.

"How about an interview with your mothers?" she asked. "They were all very fashionable when Malcolm was dating them."

"My mum's a physicist."

"I know, but she was also named one of the most beautiful women in Britain."

Steven's eyes narrowed.

"I don't see how an article on my mum will benefit me," he said.

"We could do a photo shoot with each of the women in the business units—the airline, the record label and the retail store. I mean Tiffany Malone would be a natural at Everest Records. I can see the spread already.

"We can have each of you in there in a smaller perspective—Henry is definitely on the cutting edge of fashion…and Geoff is very traditional."

"And I'm all business," Steven said.

Ainsley looked at him. At this man who'd dismissed her because she'd been frumpy and overweight and he'd made an offhand comment that had devastated her… "Maybe we could do a makeover with you at one of our sister magazines."

He quirked one eyebrow at her. "I'm not a makeover kind of guy. If we agreed to this, then it'd be an exclusive for you."

Ainsley thought about it. She'd have to talk to her team, but there had to be some way to make this happen. "I'm not sure we can fit you into our schedule. I mean, if I had Malcolm in the article, too…then that would be a coup."

"It would be. But I can't promise that Malcolm would do it."

"Not close to him?"

"He's dying, Ainsley," Steven said.

She felt a pang. He hadn't shown any emotion at all. She wondered if that meant that he was scared of losing his father and didn't want anyone to know.

"I'm so very sorry."

He nodded. "Back to business here. You finish your shoot with Jon and then do feature articles on all of us from the fashion angle involving our mums—which issue?"

"I have to get back to the office and double-check my schedule, but I think it will be in the fall."

"Very well," he said. "It's a deal."

"Great," she said, turning to walk away.

"Do you have time for dinner to discuss the details? You could let Davis and Jon finish their shoot."

Ainsley didn't want to have a dinner with him. She'd had a crush on him ever since she'd done that interview five years ago. Not a stalk-him-like-a-crazy-woman-and-lie-in-his-bushes crush, but a kind of obsession that involved reading every article published on him. Would it be a good idea to go to dinner with him? Their relationship would have to stay professional, she reminded herself.

But he'd changed her life. When she'd realized that to a man like Steven she'd been completely invisible, it was shattering. Not just because of her size, but because she hadn't kept control of the interview. He'd unnerved the woman she'd been five years earlier and spurred her change. And now she wanted nothing more to do with him…well, that wasn't true. She'd love to exact a measure of revenge after the way he'd dissed her.

And she had no plans for tonight other than heading back to the office, working on page proofs and approving every detail of the magazine she'd fought so hard to become the editor-in-chief of. She could squeeze out a few hours for Steven.

"Agreed," she said.

"Should we shake hands and have a contract drawn up?" he asked.

"What?"

"For our dinner. You make it sound like an all-day meeting you're dreading. I think that dinner with me will be enjoyable."

He was confident and she remembered his charm only too well. "Do you think so? Can you guarantee it?"

"Indeed I can."

Her BlackBerry buzzed crazily with text messages and e-mail notifications. She glanced down at the screen. At least three fires demanded her attention. "When and where for dinner?"

She motioned for Davis's assistant to come over.

"Nine. I'll pick you up."

"That's not necessary. I'd rather drive myself."

"I'm not sure where I can get a reservation with this late notice. Give me your address," he said.

She realized that Steven was used to getting his way, which was interesting because she was, too. She thought about digging her heels in on this issue, but time was money and they'd lost enough today waiting for someone to clean up this mess.

"Fine. You can pick me up at my office," she said, and then rattled off the address.

"See you then," he said and turned to leave. She watched him walk away, admiring the swagger in his step. He was a fine-looking man from the back, she thought, noticing the way his dress pants cupped his butt when he took a step.

"Are we okay to work?" Joanie asked. Joanie was Ainsley's age and had been working for Davis for the last ten years. She was slim and tall and her striking features made Ainsley think that Joanie could have been a model. But the other woman preferred to work behind the camera instead of in front of it.

"I believe we are."

"Great. I'll go get Jon back into makeup and let Davis know," Joanie said. "This was about to be one expensive mistake."

Ainsley needed no reminding. She waved over Danielle Bridges, the editor in charge of this article. Ainsley was here for star management and she was very glad she'd been here today. Danielle was new on their staff and Ainsley had yet to determine if she could hold her own.

"I am so sorry about this. I spoke to the manager several times to confirm the details," Danielle said.

The other woman had been apologizing all morning. "We can talk about this later. The issue has been resolved and we are going to get some great photos to go with the fabulous article you edited," Ainsley said. She believed that most people rose to challenges when they felt their superiors believed in them. And she also believed in reprimanding people in private.

"Thanks," Danielle said.

A minute later a twenty-something girl with stick-straight blond hair walked up to her. "Mr. Devonshire asked that I assist you in whatever you need. I'm Anne."

"You can work with Joanie."

Ainsley and Danielle stood off to the side, with Ainsley answering e-mails on her BlackBerry and waiting until she was sure the photo shoot was underway. Then she left the store to go back to her office.

Frederick VonHauser was waiting in her office. He was on her staff but also a trusted friend. Freddie and she had met when they'd both been attending Northwestern. Back then Freddie had been Larry Murphy. But he'd decided that he needed a new name for his new college life and had changed it their junior year.

"Everything settled?"

"Yes. Steven Devonshire was there."

"No kidding. Did he remember you?"

"Nope. Not even a flicker of recognition. Should I fire Danielle? She didn't follow up and Davis and Jon stood around for over an hour with nothing to do. It was a complete mess."

"Darling, I know you too well to let you change the subject. Are you sure he didn't recognize you?"

"Yes. And that doesn't matter. I'm having dinner with him later this evening."

"Ains, you sneaky girl. So you were going to keep that to yourself?"

"I was. Because my underling shouldn't know every detail of my life."

"Underling? I prefer esteemed colleague."

"You are. Now about Danielle…"

"She's young. And the article she wrote is one of the best I've seen in a long time. But she's not going to learn if we don't push her."

"She cost me hundreds of thousands today, Freddie. I can't keep her on."

He looked as if he wanted to argue but didn't. She put her pen down and thought about the articles she'd agreed to run in the magazine.

"I need someone who can handle sports stars and royals."

"For what?"

"A series of articles on the Devonshire heirs and their mothers. I want to showcase all three separately and then I need someone with a connection to Malcolm Devonshire. I want to do a sit-down with all three of his sons and him. I want the angle to be on mothering."

"Good luck with that. How'd you get the heirs to agree?"

"It was Steven's price for getting back to the photo shoot."

"You and Steven made all kinds of deals, didn't you?"

"Yes, I did."

"Ains, was that wise? The man left you devastated before," Freddie said.

"I have no idea, but when I realized he didn't remember me and that he was interested in me now…"

She trailed off. She couldn't say that a part of her wanted revenge. That wasn't very noble and she knew she wouldn't do anything to hurt Steven. But if they had dinner and he found himself more attracted to her, and this time if she was the one to walk away without glancing back…well, then she'd be just fine with that.

"Girl, this has disaster written all over it. You emerged from the ashes the last time as a phoenix, but that kind of transformation can't happen twice in a lifetime."

"Says who?"

He shrugged. "I guess you have to do what you think is right."

"It's not that," she said. "I'm just curious."

"Curious about a man who left you so shattered that you lost a ton of weight and had to move to another continent to recover? That kind of curiosity could be more than you can handle."

She just looked at Freddie. She wasn't going to back out of the date. She'd made up her mind that this time she'd emerge the victor from her encounter with Steven. A few minutes later Freddie left the office and she sat back in her chair. She didn't want to think too much about her deal with Steven or that it had nothing to do with this magazine and everything to do with the man—Steven Devonshire.

Two

Ainsley fidgeted nervously as she looked at herself in the bathroom mirror. Sometimes she still saw the fat girl she'd once been looking back at her. She turned to her side and stared at her stomach. That carb fest she'd indulged in at lunch had been a mistake. She was going to have to have a veggie soup for dinner.

She glanced at the slim-fitting black skirt. She was always torn when she looked at her reflection. She liked the body she saw in the mirror, but she never felt at home in it. She kept expecting the image to balloon up like one of those carnival mirrors she'd seen at the county fair growing up in Florida.

Sometimes she was really struck by how far she'd come. At times she could scarcely recall the small-town girl she had been, but at other times she felt just as awkward and out of place as ever.

The bathroom door opened, she put on her power smile and leaned in as if she'd just been checking her lipstick. It was Danielle. The other woman stared at her.

"I thought we were cool," Danielle said.

Ainsley shook her head. "I'm sorry, but that cost us a lot of money today and now I have to go in front of my bosses and get them to sign off on another idea."

"I know that I dropped the ball, but I'm just learning," Danielle said.

"When I was just learning, Danielle, I lost my job for making a mistake like you. It took me three years to get my career back on track," Ainsley said. The botched interview with Steven had cost her her job with the *Business Journal*.

"Then give me a break here. You know how hard it is to start over."

"That's right, I do. So I don't make major mistakes anymore. I'm not sure you learned from this one."

Danielle crossed her arms over her chest. "How about a probation period? Let's say six months of a trial and I'll prove myself to you. If I screw up again, I'll walk away and if I don't I get to stay on full time."

Ainsley realized that Danielle had gumption. She was an incredibly talented editor, if Ainsley was forced to admit it. "Okay, it's a deal. But don't make me regret it."

"I won't."

Ainsley walked out of the ladies' restroom to see Freddie leaning against the wall. "Did you put her up to that?"

"Yes, I did. I think we haven't seen the best of her yet and if she wanted a second chance, I told her she'd have to go and make you give her one."

She glanced over at her oldest friend. "You are so lucky I like you."

He kissed her cheek. "I know. When do you talk to New York about your idea for the Devonshire heirs story?"

Even though Ainsley was editor-in-chief for *FQ*, she still answered to her boss in New York. They were owned by the best-selling magazine consortium in the world, and her boss liked to say they were number one because he was so hands-on.

"In an hour. I had to squeeze it onto the agenda at the end of the video conference call. I would love to have some photos of the women from when they were all dating Malcolm," she said. "Do you think you can get on Corbis and find them?"

"I can and I will. What else do you need?"

"Nothing. I'll do my other research, but finding the photos would be time-consuming. I need them to be unique and glamorous..."

"I think I know what you have in mind. I'll e-mail them to you as soon as I have them."

"Thanks, Freddie," she said.

"I owe you one after I sicced Danielle on you."

"This doesn't make up for that."

"What does?"

"A jog along the Thames tomorrow morning at seven."

"Seven? That's still the middle of the night," he said.

"But you owe me, so you'll be there."

"You're right, I will be," he said. He headed down the hall to his own office and she reentered hers.

It was one thing to think of doing a story of this magnitude, but it was something else entirely to convince her publisher that it should be done. And she needed to make sure they could do the story she'd proposed.

She spent the next hour pulling up details on the women

who had been involved with Malcolm Devonshire. And Ainsley was fascinated by what she'd found. The women were all very dynamic and, from a fashion perspective, she couldn't have asked for three women whose sense of style was more distinctive and individual. There was Henry's mother, Tiffany Malone—the embodiment of a seventies hippie chick rocker. With her sexy long hair, sultry eyes and pencil-slim jeans, she was earthy and radiated sexuality. It was hard to think of her as being someone's mum.

Then there was Princess Louisa—the wild-child party girl who was a distant cousin of the current monarch. Her look was haute-couture sexiness from her stick-straight bob to her slim-fitting, low-cut tops and hip-hugging slacks. She was glamour with a capital *G*.

Then there was Lynn Grandings—Steven's mother. The physicist, who should have seemed very much like a bookworm, but instead radiated a keen intelligence and with her waist-length, thick, curly brown hair, she exuded her own brand of sexuality. The picture that Freddie had sent showed her laughing at the camera, and it was easy to see why Malcolm had been attracted to her.

The only thing the women had in common was a distinctive beauty all their own. These women were defined by their lifestyles and she was dying to know what had attracted Malcolm to them at the same time. How had he been able to juggle these relationships?

She finished making her notes and realized that talking to the sons would be the perfect accompaniment for the story because these strong women raised them.

Dinah sat across from him in the conference room. He'd ordered the financials for Everest Mega Stores from the last three years. The retail stores had suffered a setback over the last quarter but even prior to that there had been signs of decline. The pattern that emerged showed that the North American retail stores were the ones that were having the most problems.

"I think our North American retail shops should be closed," Steven said after he finished reading the financials.

"I'm not sure," Dinah said. "If we do that we stop the loss, but we aren't going to see a new revenue stream."

"If we focus our energies here," he said, gesturing to the spreadsheet for Europe and the UK, "I think we can make it up. But I'm open to ideas on how to keep North America. I don't really want to lose that market."

"Why don't I do some research? I can write a report on the analysis of closing the North American stores versus keeping them open. I'll recommend some course of action as well, if you like."

Steven glanced over at Dinah. "I like that idea. Can you have it to me by Friday?"

"Close of business?"

"If you need that long," he said.

"Yes. I might take all the time."

"I don't mind. I want to make sure we're doing the right thing."

Dinah stood up and gathered her purse and briefcase. "We will. You're known for saving companies like this one, so it should be a piece of cake."

"Exactly."

"Is that why you took this job?" she asked.

Steven shrugged. Dinah and he had worked together a long time and never had the conversations turned personal. They sometimes flirted and always talked business and market trends, but never did any conversation broach the personal areas of their lives.

"Off-limits?" she asked.

"No. This is business—pure and simple," he said. Opting for the truth as he saw it. The inheritance issues weren't a big thing for him, because he saw this as a challenge and the chance to prove himself was too great for him to pass up.

"Good. I'm going to let my phone go to voice mail tonight."

"You are? Why?"

She flushed and for the first time he realized that Dinah had a life outside the office. He always suspected she must, but they did work almost sixty hours a week so that didn't leave much time for dating.

"I have a date and he told me to turn the phone off at dinner tonight if I wanted to see him again," she said, her voice quiet and a little pensive.

"Okay, voice mail is fine. In fact, take the entire evening off. I don't want you returning calls until tomorrow."

"Does midnight count as tomorrow?"

He laughed. She was still his workaholic Dinah. "Of course it does."

Dinah left a few minutes later and Steven sat back in his chair thinking about Ainsley Patterson. There had been something familiar about her, but he would have remembered meeting her.

He made plans for dinner and then started going through his executive staff. He called them all in one at a time and wrote down his impressions afterward. He had a list of people he thought were go-getters and could move the company forward. Unfortunately, there was a list of people who saw their job here as a paycheck only. He'd have to move them around and see if that sparked some enthusiasm. Otherwise he'd have to fire them.

No matter the outcome, it was only a matter of time before he had this company running like a well-oiled machine.

He wasn't sure when it had happened—perhaps when he'd been a boy playing quietly in the sterile environment of his mother's lab—but he'd always known that he could rely on no one but himself.

Three

Steven had to detour back to the Leicester Square store to fire that duty manager. He had his secretary send a message to his half brothers that he'd be late meeting them. It was odd to think that these men he'd known about his entire life but had never met were now such an integral part of it. He wasn't too sure how he felt about that. He didn't necessarily want brothers.

He'd never yearned for a family as a child and as an adult he'd found that making his own way in the world suited him. Family just hadn't been part of his reality. His mum was always in the lab, and Aunt Lucy was busy with her life.

His cell rang and he glanced down to see that it was his aunt Lucy. Lucy was his mother's twin, the nurturer in their family. She called him once a week to just check on him.

Aunt Lucy had tried to mother him, but Steven had always known she was doing it because she didn't think his mum was. And that left Steven feeling…cold.

"Aunt Lucy."

"Hello, Steven. How are you doing, dear?"

"I'm good. How are you?"

"Fine, dear. I heard from your mother that your father had contacted you."

Steven sighed as he exited his building. He went to his car—a Vallerio roadster. He had an original 1969 model in his garage at home. The new roadster had all the earmarks of the original, but power for this new millennium.

"It was nothing. He wants me to run one of his business units."

"And the others?"

Others. That was how his mum and Aunt Lucy referred to his half brothers. Was it any wonder he'd never been close to them?

"They are each running a segment as well. Whoever outperforms the others will be made the CEO of the Everest Group."

"Sounds like your kind of challenge, dear. Will you be able to come home to Oxford on Sunday for dinner?"

He hesitated for a second. Not because he was considering it, but he wanted her to think he was. His aunt meant well and she was the only one of his relatives he talked to on a regular basis, so he always made the effort of at least seeming to want to spend time with her.

"Not this week."

"Oh, well, maybe another time. Have a good evening."

"You, too, Aunt Lucy."

He hung up and got in the car. He drove through the

congested London streets to the Athenaeum Club. The members-only club would afford them the privacy they needed to talk. To have a chance to get to know each other away from the prying eyes of the paparazzi. Steven wasn't used to the spotlight the way that Henry and Geoff were. But it didn't bother him. He was enough of a businessman to know that any publicity was good.

In this day and age anything could be spun. He had made a dinner reservation for him and Ainsley at an African restaurant that he liked. He pulled up to the front of the club and the valet came to take his keys.

"I know I'm not a member," a young woman said to the butler guarding the door. "I just need to send a message to Henry Devonshire. I know he's in here."

"I can relay a message for you," Steven said. "I'm meeting him inside."

"I just need to speak to him for a moment. Will you let him know I'm out here?"

"I sure will," Steven said, smiling at the woman as she stepped aside. "And who are you?"

"Astrid Taylor."

Steven nodded to her and then turned to the butler. "Steven Devonshire," he said.

"Of course, sir," he said. The door was opened for him and he entered the club.

The centuries-old club was decorated in a very conservative manner and it was lined with tables and chairs in discreet groupings. There was a bar at one end of the room and he spotted Henry and Geoff sitting at one of the tables toward the back.

"There's a girl asking for you up front," he said by way of greeting to Henry.

The other men and he shared little in the way of looks.

Geoff dressed like he was part of the upper crust of society, which he was. Henry always looked spot-on trendy, which made sense because he spent so much time with the people who made the trends that others followed.

"A girl?" Henry asked.

"Astrid," he said. "I told them I'd let you know."

"Thanks," Henry said. He put his glass on the table and stood up. "Sorry to miss chatting with you, Steven. I need to go."

"Do you?" Geoff asked. "Who is she?"

"My new assistant, Astrid Taylor."

Steven signaled the butler and ordered a Seagram's Seven. It was an old-fashioned drink, but one he'd always favored. The conversation went on between the other two men, talking about families and their half-siblings, and Steven felt distinctly uncomfortable. He had no family except his mum and Aunt Lucy. And he certainly didn't want to talk about them. Steven found it interesting that Henry and Geoff's mums had remarried and created families for their sons.

After Henry left, Steven sat back in his chair to assess Geoff's mood. "How's the airline business?"

"A mess. I'm not sure that this 'boon' from Malcolm is much of a gift. The airline is on shaky ground and the baggage handlers are threatening to strike. I have some ideas for turning it around, but it will be hard work. How about the retail stores?"

Steven had heard rumors about the airline within business circles. "The retail chain is healthy in Europe and here in the UK, but the North American division is faltering. I wonder how Malcolm let the business get into such bad shape?"

Geoff shrugged. "His obsession with flying around the

globe probably contributed to it. Or, as we all know, his obsession with women."

Steven couldn't help but chuckle. At the end of the day that might be what had cost Malcolm the cutting edge he'd had when he was younger. That was a mistake that Steven was determined not to make.

He liked to think he'd gotten the best skills from both his parents. From his mother, Lynn Grandings, a Nobel Prize-winning physicist, he'd learned to apply the scientific method to every aspect of his life and to be methodical about planning, but he'd also been introduced to some of his mum's crazy ideas. She always said that progress was made from ideas that others thought were...whacked. And from Malcolm he'd learned that winning at all costs was the most important thing.

"I forgot to mention to Henry that I have made arrangements for *Fashion Quarterly* to interview our mothers and us."

"What? Why would a fashion magazine be interested in us?" Geoff asked.

"Our mums were all very fashionable women in their day and the editor-in-chief thinks that you and Henry are fashion-forward now. She's going to do photo shoots of each us with our mums near something related to our business units. The editor-in-chief wants to assign a writer to interview all three of us and Malcolm. I'm not sure what his health is like, so I don't know if that will be possible."

"I'm not too keen on talking about myself and I don't know that my mum will agree, but the airline could use a boost. As long as they stick to that angle, I'll do it."

"Good. I'll have my assistant send the details. And now I have to go."

"Me, too," Geoff said. "Thanks for dropping by."

"You're welcome. I guess it's time we got to know each other."

"Past time," Geoff said.

The men walked out together and there were photographers waiting outside. Steven stayed back and watched the mayhem that surrounded Geoff. There were questions about his distant cousins, the royal princes, and questions about his mother. All of which Geoff brushed off as he walked to his own car, ignoring the photographers.

After the pack of paparazzi had left, Steven left as the valet brought his car to the front. After meeting with his half brothers, he knew he was going to win the challenge that Malcolm had thrown down, but he wondered if it would fill the empty hole in his soul.

The restaurant that Steven had chosen was classy, but had a homey atmosphere. The décor was distinctly African and the lighting was low, offering them a sense of privacy.

The details of the interviews weren't something she could talk about with him now. She had to talk to her staff writers and she wanted to see if Freddie could line up an interview with Malcolm before she made any decisions.

"Thank you for letting us go ahead with our shoot. I'm sure I don't need to tell you how much it cost us to just wait around."

"You're very welcome," Steven said. He'd ordered a bottle of white African wine to go with their dinner and lifted a glass to toast after the sommelier had brought it to them and Steven had approved it.

"To winning combinations," he said.

She nodded and tipped the bell of her glass toward him. Their glasses clinked together and she looked into his eyes as she took her first sip. He watched her the entire time, which she thought was interesting. He seemed like someone who was shallow and only concerned about his own needs, but he was definitely paying attention to her. He watched every expression on her face and she felt as if he wanted to make sure she enjoyed herself tonight. That was out of character for the man she'd met five years ago.

A bouquet of flavor erupted on her tongue as she swirled the sip of wine though her mouth. It was crisp and dry and had the subtle flavor of fruit to it. Not grapes but maybe apple, she thought.

When she returned her glass to the table, she smiled at him. "I like this wine. Thank you for recommending it."

"Well, it has a bite, so I thought it might suit you."

She had to laugh at the way he said it. She knew she came across as a man-eater when she was in business mode. But tonight she wanted to enjoy the opportunity to just get to know Steven.

"You mentioned earlier that your father was sick," she said.

"I don't like to talk about Malcolm," he said.

She made a mental note that he referred to his father as Malcolm. Were they close? Somehow she didn't think that question was appropriate. As an American in London, she'd learned quickly that some of the conversational topics she'd always thought acceptable weren't here.

"My dad had a health scare about six years ago…and it really shook me. I'd always thought of him as invincible and it was humbling to realize he wasn't."

"Yes, it can be hard," Steven said. "My mother is healthy as can be but she spends a lot of time in a sterile environment, so that's to be expected."

"What does she do?" Ainsley asked. She had done

her research on Lynn but wanted to hear about her from Steven.

A frown crossed his face so quickly that if she hadn't been watching him she would have missed it. "My mother is a physicist. She's won a few awards. Right now she's working in Switzerland."

"I guess you don't see her often," Ainsley said.

The waiter brought their dinners and they continued to discuss their families. It didn't take long for her to notice that Steven always deflected the questions she asked about his family. Not that it mattered—her writers would get to him.

"What brought you to London?" he asked as they were sipping a darkly brewed after-dinner coffee.

She wondered if he'd remember her if she mentioned the interview she'd done with him. It was that article that had ultimately cost her her job. She'd been so nervous when she'd met Steven at his office that she'd spilled her coffee all over his desk. He'd been cordial to her at the time but when she left she overheard him on the phone with Joel, her boss. Heard him say that she'd been more concerned about her coffee and sweet snack than about interviewing him. When she got back to her office, it hadn't surprised her that her boss fired her.

She'd written the article anyway and sent it out freelance to a couple of magazines, finally getting it picked up by one of the *Business Journal*'s competitors. It had appeared in *WIRED* magazine; they had been looking for articles on "young guns"—men under thirty who were changing and shaping the way businesses were being managed. That article put her on the map, so to speak, and gave her a chance to start fresh.

She was a little miffed Steven hadn't recognized her

name but remembered that back then she'd been A. J. Patterson—something she'd thought made her seem more professional.

"My job. I used to work as a freelance writer in the States. But it's hard to pay the bills with freelance gigs only, so I transitioned to an editor position at *Fashion Quarterly* in the States. While I was there, a piece I wrote on young Hollywood wowed my bosses and they offered me a full-time position as an editor. Once I started editing—which is very different than writing—I found that I loved it."

"As much as writing?" he asked.

She shrugged, but then she decided, why not tell him. "Some days but what I loved about writing was the discovery, digging deeper and asking questions that surprised the people being interviewed. Not in a bad way, but just in a way that pushed them to examine and expand their own responses. I liked that."

"Do you write anymore?" he asked.

No one ever thought to ask her that, she observed. The truth was there were times when she did miss writing but being an editor, especially one in her position, paid so much better. "No, I don't. I'm in charge of our entire magazine."

"Do you like being the boss?" he asked.

"Love it," she said, with a grin.

She hadn't realized until she'd gotten a full-time position at *FQ* that she really loved the competitive nature of her industry. It had also helped her focus on staying healthy. Working in fashion had made her very aware that she had to make her weight loss a permanent thing.

"But enough about me. You must be looking for a huge challenge to take on the Everest Mega Stores on top of running Raleighvale China. Or have you stepped down there?"

"No, I haven't stepped down. I don't think I ever will. Raleighvale is in my blood."

"How?" she asked. He was more open when she asked him about business. That was another interesting note that she mentally tucked away to examine later.

"It's my own company. I took it over when I was young and made it into the success it is today. There's a certain sense of pride of ownership that comes with that."

She nodded. "I'd heard you took over the company from your grandfather."

"Indeed. I was looking for something to do after college."

"Did you bum around Europe?" she asked. She couldn't see that. Steven didn't seem like the type of man who would be able to just drift.

"No. I spent a few years mining in Staffordshire learning about Raleighvale. When Grandfather wanted to retire, I jumped at the challenge it represented."

She thought about that. About what it said about Steven that he was the kind of man who could take a few years to do mining. That was tough work. Not the kind of job she would have expected Malcolm Devonshire's son to do.

"What did Malcolm say about that?" she asked.

"I have no idea. I didn't ask him."

She nodded. Her father hadn't wanted her to move to New York when she'd taken her first magazine job, and when she'd moved to London, he'd been upset as well. But her parents never hesitated to say what was on their mind. In the end they'd understood that she needed her career. Her mother was always asking if a man had broken her heart and Ainsley always changed the subject. Because

Steven had broken her heart, but not in a romantic way. He'd done it on a much bigger scale and it had completely changed the woman she had been.

They were small-town folks—mail carriers. Well, her mum now worked mostly at the counter in the local post office. A small branch where she knew just about everyone's name who came in there.

"I guess that's a good thing," she said.

He signaled the waiter and asked for the check. She took her platinum card from her wallet, intending to split the check, but he gave her a look that made her pull it back.

"This isn't a date," she said.

"Who said?"

Steven found that behind the slim-fitting clothes and the underlying sexuality of her Betty Page look, Ainsley was a very interesting woman. He wanted to know more about her. He wanted to spend all night talking to her and listening to the way she spoke. He liked her insights and the way she looked at him. For once, he felt as if he were a hollow shell of a man. A man who had only one dimension: business.

But with Ainsley...well, she made him wonder if he had been wrong to keep such a distance between himself and others.

Or maybe this was just the first blush of attraction—that potent combination of lust and intrigue. She was a mystery to him. A woman unlike others he'd met and seduced.

In her there was a sort of innocence—she seemed to be unaware of her appeal to the opposite sex. Men stared at her as she preceded him out of the restaurant, but she ignored their looks. He glared at one man who stared too long and then put his hand on the small of her back.

She was with him. He was glad that he'd thought to bargain for her magazine to do the articles on him and Henry and Geoff because he wanted to have a reason to keep in touch with her.

He was going to ask her out again—that was a given. He needed to have her in his bed. He wanted to see if her mysteries would be solved by making love. He'd found in the past that the appeal of a lot of the women he'd dated vanished after he'd bedded them.

That wouldn't be the same with Ainsley. And yet a part of him believed that it would be. That she'd be like every other relationship in his life. He was used to expecting nothing from them.

"Why are you helping me walk out of the restaurant?" she asked.

"So every man in the place knows that you are with me."

"Am I with you, Steven?"

"Yes, you are."

"Just for tonight?"

"No. I want to have you by my side again. I have to go to a reception for my mother next Tuesday evening at Oxford. Would you like to accompany me?"

They stepped out into the March evening. It was damp and chilly and Ainsley shivered. If they had a different kind of relationship, he would have wrapped his arm around her. But then, he thought, to hell with that. He put his arm over her shoulder and drew her against the curve of his body.

She shuddered and looked up at him.

He read the same desire in her expression that he'd been battling all night. Her deep violet eyes revealed that she was thinking of him as a man—not an interviewee—and he knew that he'd do anything to keep that interest alive.

With the gentle pressure of his arm on her shoulder, he steered her down the street to where he'd parked his car. When they got to his car, she stopped and turned, trapped between his body and his vehicle.

"What do you want from me?" she asked. Her voice was soft and low. There was none of the confident executive that he'd first met in the Everest Mega Store this afternoon. Instead, there was a woman who showed him a hint of vulnerability. And that touched him.

He brushed the softer emotions aside—he didn't like them. He touched the rounded apples of her cheeks, ran his finger over that arch down toward her ear. "Right now I want a kiss."

"Just one?" she asked. She licked her lips, a slow sensual movement of her tongue that made him groan inside. Her tongue was delicate and pink and he wanted to feel it on his skin. He wanted her to taste him the same way. And he needed to taste her in return.

With those full lips and her sexy smile… What would she taste like?

"To start," he said.

He traced the line of her neck with his fingertip and along the hairline of her high ponytail where her hair met her skin. She shivered a little and licked her lips again. Then she leaned toward him, not close enough that their bodies brushed, but closer.

He kept his light touch on her face. Just taking his time. All the best things in life took time. He'd never gone for instant gratification, but this time he was tempted to. He made himself wait, though. Patience always paid off.

He traced the vee at the top of her blouse. Her breasts were large, full and he didn't come close to touching them, but he wanted to. Instead, he contented himself with the soft tender skin of her chest, that area exposed by her blouse.

Then he leaned toward her and she tipped her head back and went up on her toes. He looked down into her upturned face. Her eyes were half closed and he had that momentary surge of lust that always assailed him when he was close to tasting a new woman.

She put her hands on his shoulders as he hesitated, drawing out the moment, and lifted herself even higher so that he felt the brush of her warm breath against his mouth. But he pulled back.

He would decide when they had their first kiss. He would set the tone and the timbre of the embrace. And he wanted to make sure that Ainsley knew he was in charge.

Starting where he'd first touched her with his finger, he followed the same path with his lips, caressing his way with nibbling kisses to her ear.

He blew gently into her ear. "Do you want me?"

"Yes…"

"Good."

Four

There was nothing she could do but Steven's bidding. She'd lost all sense of place and self as he touched her face. She knew that she'd do whatever he asked her to as long as he kept touching her. If only he'd kiss her. She wanted to feel that firm hard mouth against her own.

But he kept teasing her. When he bit her ear, she gasped his name and felt a bolt of pure desire go through her. Her breasts felt fuller, her blood raced through her veins and between her legs she felt moisture as her body readied itself for him.

Which was ridiculous—she wasn't about to sleep with Steven Devonshire. Or was she? She might, she thought. Immediately, her mind focused on the potential conflict of interest created by the article. The writer would simply mention that she and Steven…what? Slept together? She knew that would hurt the journalistic integrity of the piece, but the article was really more focused on the mothers.

Before she could ruminate on it any more, she felt his mouth on her neck. He ran a line of kisses down the length of her neck and then at the base she felt the warmth of his tongue. She shuddered again.

When she'd lost weight, she'd had a reawakening of herself as a woman, but the attention of men had been too much. Now she realized it was the wrong men who had been paying attention to her. Because in Steven's embrace she felt that she was where she was meant to be.

He whispered hot, dark words against her skin, which just served to inflame her. She reached for his shoulders, tried to draw him closer to her, but he pulled back.

"Do not touch me until I tell you to," he said.

"Why not?"

"Because I said so," he said.

She dropped her hands to her sides, but had no idea what to do with them. Letting him touch her while she couldn't touch him was exciting. She felt like this moment was all about her pleasure and all he'd done was kiss her. The wind blew down the street chilly and damp, and she realized they were standing on the side of the road.

Until that instant all she'd been focused on was his kiss. A kiss she still hadn't tasted.

"Let's get inside the car," she said.

"Not until I get my kiss," Steven said.

She started to argue but then felt his mouth against her collarbone. He'd brushed the fabric of her shirt out of his way, as he tasted her with short kisses. His mouth was warm and started a fire that raged all the way to her core.

She had the uncomfortable feeling that she might not

be able to deny him anything. His moved his mouth up the other side of her blouse and then at the base of her neck he suckled her. She shivered and moaned as an ache started at her center.

She couldn't believe that he'd turned her into a mass of needing and wanting and she didn't care. She wanted more of him. She reached up to touch him, but he lifted one eyebrow at her and she knew that if she touched him he'd stop. She moaned and put her hands back down beside her hips.

He smiled at her. "Good girl. You get a reward for that."

She smiled back at him. "Do I get to choose it?"

He shook his head and brought his mouth down on hers. His kiss was as intense as she'd expected it to be. His mouth was hard on hers and demanded everything she had to give.

His hands circled her waist and drew her against his body. She felt the hard wall of his chest against her breasts and the hot pressure of his tongue as it penetrated her mouth. She shifted in his arms, trying to get closer to him, but she could only touch him where he let her.

Her powerlessness—to her own passion and to Steven's control—was the headiest feeling she'd ever had. His mouth was delicious. His taste was addicting. She wanted so much more than this.

Everything in her called for her to be with him. She caught his lower lip in between her teeth as he drew his mouth back from hers. He moaned and then changed the embrace so that her lips were caught between his teeth. He sucked her lower lip deeper into his mouth.

One of his big hands moved up her back to the center,

right between her shoulder blades, and he held her with just that one hand and his mouth on hers.

She was completely his prisoner. Nothing mattered to her except that this moment didn't end. That his mouth stayed on hers.

And that frightened her. This embrace scared her. She was successful because she didn't let men or relationships of any kind interfere with her job. And that had always been easy for her, because no man she'd met had threatened that resolve.

Part of it she imagined was simply because no other man had felt right—the way that Steven did. He'd been the one to change her with that one overheard comment. And she'd realized that even though her parents had always told her they loved her and she was beautiful the way she was, that men saw that differently. That a chubby woman was almost invisible to most men—or rather to men like Steven.

She had to be careful, because the way she felt right now, she knew she could easily lose herself to him. In him. And the really scary part was that she wouldn't mind. She drew back from him and he slowly released her mouth.

She put her fingers over her lower lip, which was still tingling. She wasn't herself. This was surreal.

"That was…"

"Incredible?"

She shook her head. There was a lightness to his tone that she wanted to embrace but she sensed the steel underneath. "Intense."

"Surely a woman like you has been well-kissed before."

She started to shake her head but she didn't want Steven to remember the chubby girl no man had been interested in.

That was part of her past, she thought. His kiss had made her vulnerable enough. She didn't want to show him that kind of emotional vulnerability.

"Nothing like that," she said at last. She couldn't lie to him about that. She wasn't a very sophisticated woman when it came to bedroom matters. She might be able to hold her own with temperamental photographers and celebrities, but with this man she couldn't. And she wasn't going to pretend that this was an everyday occurrence, even if that would have been better for her.

Ainsley sat quietly next to him as he drove through the city to her home. She lived in the posh neighborhood of Notting Hill. "What made you choose this area to live?"

She flushed and looked over at him. "The movie with Julia Roberts and Hugh Grant. They made it look charming and quaint."

"Is that how you decided to become a magazine editor? You saw someone in a movie doing it?"

She shrugged. "There are worse ways to find a job. What about you?"

"Not so fast. You didn't tell me why you chose your profession."

"You can park there on the street." She pointed to a space halfway down the block.

He pulled into the spot and turned the car off, but he made no move to get out and neither did she. "Which movie was it?"

"*His Girl Friday.* Have you ever seen it?"

He hadn't. He wasn't much of a film buff. He'd spent his life out doing things. Trying to prove he was better than his ancestry, and most days he was sure he succeeded.

"No. What's it about?"

"A newspaper editor—Cary Grant and his ex-wife and star reporter Rosalind Russell…it's just great. They made working at a newspaper look like so much fun. I knew I wanted to be a reporter."

"But you're not," he pointed out.

"Once I graduated I found a different path. But I would never have thought of writing for a living if not for that movie."

She sparkled with passion when she talked about writing and he wondered why she'd given it up. He knew she'd said that the new job better suited her but he still couldn't believe she'd give up her passion for money.

"How old were you when you made the decision to be a writer?"

"Twelve," she said. "What about you? Did you decide early on that you wanted to rule the world?"

He laughed out loud at her wry question. "Pretty much from the womb I knew I wanted it all."

"Do you think you've gotten it?" she asked.

He tipped his head to the side to study her. She asked questions that no one else ever had—except that one reporter. The frumpy, clumsy woman had little in common with Ainsley except for her eyes and her probing questions. He remembered the woman's eyes…so similar to Ainsley's.

"Not yet, but I'm close," he said.

He tried to recall other details of the woman but he couldn't see anything but those wide violet eyes. He took his keys from the ignition and got out of the car to come around and open her door.

One thing his mother had been a stickler about was manners in a man. She said that women liked to be treated with respect and that they always deserved it.

He'd often wondered if Malcolm's betrayal with his other mistresses had wounded his mum deeply. She'd buried herself in her lab and in her research after his birth. Steven could think of no greater disrespect than finding out the man you were having an affair with was seeing two other women at the same time.

He opened her door and offered his hand. She took it, her fingers small and delicate in his bigger grasp. She turned in her seat, stretching her legs out the door first. They were slim and yet curvy, one of the first things he'd noticed about her. Once she had one foot on the sidewalk, she stepped out and stood next to him. He wanted her again. Wanted to kiss her once more, but he knew better than to move too quickly.

He wanted to savor every moment with her. To make this quasi-emotion he felt—one he knew was lust—last a little while longer before he went back to the dull, gray world he usually inhabited. The world where he just worked and concentrated on proving he was the best.

"I'll see you to your door," he said.

"That's not necessary," she said. "I think I can find it."

"I insist."

He put his hand on the small of her back again and nudged her toward her door. She tossed that high ponytail of hers as she looked back over her shoulder at him. "You don't take no for an answer, do you?"

"Not unless I have to. Men who back down usually end up losing."

"I don't like to lose, either," she said.

"If you want what I want, then we'll both win."

"Somehow I'm not sure I'll know if I really want it or if your will has made me think I do," she said.

Her words had been carefully chosen. She was trying to tell him that he overwhelmed her, or at least that was what he suspected.

"I'm not going to ask for anything you're not ready for," he said.

She studied him for a moment and he hoped she found whatever it was she was searching for. Hoped she didn't see that emptiness he always tried to mask. That spot inside him where he suspected other people had their hearts but he just had a driving impulse to succeed.

"Would you like to come in for a drink?" she asked.

"I'd love to," he walked behind her to her front door, keeping his hand on the small of her back the entire time.

Her waist was small and pronounced, her hips larger but not too big. He brought his other hand to her waist because he wanted to see what his hands looked like on her body. He really wanted to hold her like this when she was naked. To see the full curves of her bare derrière.

"What are you doing?"

"Imagining you naked," he said.

She blushed and dropped her keys. She bent to pick them up and he moaned as the fabric of her skirt was pulled taut against her buttocks. He let his hands slide down her curves, skimming along the outside of her hips until he almost reached the hem of the skirt.

She stood up, put her key in the lock and opened the door. "Don't do that."

"Why not?"

"Because we still have a business arrangement. A deal for me to publish feature articles about your family—we shouldn't have a personal relationship on top of that."

"We aren't working together, Ainsley," he said, stepping

over her threshold and forcing her to take a step back. He closed the door behind them and leaned forward to cage her against the wall.

"What we have is so much more than a business arrangement," he said.

"Really?" she asked. "Because it seems to me that you're the type of man who'll only say that until you've been in my bed."

Ainsley was seduced by everything about Steven. He was a charming dinner companion and he knew how to pay attention to a woman. He leaned in when she spoke, listened to her answers and then asked her questions that invited her to talk more deeply. It was something that no other man had done when she'd been out with him.

But this feeling was similar to ones he'd evoked in her before. And after those short few hours spent together talking, he'd left and ruined her life.

With this new body she knew that men found her attractive. It was silly to say but she still felt like the chubby girl who sat in the back of the classroom alone. She doubted that was going to change anytime soon.

Having Steven's attention wasn't going to make it easier. Yet she wanted him. She wanted to be the kind of sophisticated woman who could take him to her bed and have no regrets if he walked away in the morning.

But she wasn't. He was so close to her that she could feel his body heat. His hands were on either side of the wall next to her head. He surrounded her.

She glanced up at him, trying once again to see something in his eyes that would tell her what kind of man he was. All night long she'd asked probing questions—used her best reporter's techniques from the old days—and she'd gotten nothing from him.

A few answers to a few questions, but nothing that she could hang her hat on.

"What is going on in that head of yours?" he asked. His tone so very British that she wanted to melt. She loved the accent, so different from her soft Southern twang.

"I'm trying to gauge the measure of the man before me."

Steven didn't move, but she felt as if he'd stepped closer to her. His left hand shifted slightly on the wall and he stroked her cheekbone with his thumb.

His touch was electric. She'd realized that earlier when he'd kissed her by his car. She was powerless against it. No man had ever touched her like that before. No man had ever made her feel...sexy.

She realized then that there was no way she would turn him away. He was the first man to look at her since she'd lost all her weight and made her feel like she was a woman.

"Have I come up lacking?" he asked.

"No, Steven, you haven't," she said.

"I like the sound of my name on your lips," he said.

"Really? Why?"

His thumb moved lower on her face caressing her lower lip as he stared down at her. She was glad she'd left the light on in the living room because it cast a soft glow in the foyer.

"Your voice softens when you use my name. Otherwise, you're all business," he said.

In the quiet of her foyer she felt safe admitting the truth to him. "My job is my life."

He arched one eyebrow at her. "The same has been said of me."

"And is it true?"

He shrugged. "Many believe it is. But I have other interests."

"Like what?" she asked, hoping to learn something that she hadn't read online or in a magazine. Steven Devonshire raised privacy to an altogether new level.

"Skydiving."

That took her completely by surprise. Skydiving was a risky venture, despite the safety measures taken by everyone who participated in the sport. By the same token, she could see the appeal in the sport for Steven. He thrived on risk and excitement.

No one else would have taken on the challenge of Raleighvale China the way he had, she mused. But that was part of his personality. Ainsley knew he liked the challenge of knowing everyone expected him to fail and then shocking the hell out of them. She had first picked up on that when she'd interviewed him years ago.

"What about you, Ms. Editor-in-Chief? What do you do for fun?"

"Read," she said.

"Reading? That's not doing something, Ainsley," he said.

She shook her head. "You're wrong. I've lived adventures you've never dreamed of through the pages of my books. I've been places that I wouldn't be brave enough to travel to."

"Where?" he asked, still stroking his thumb over her face.

"Somalia. I read a book by a man who'd grown up there

and dealt with the violence and danger to the people still living there."

"I'd have to agree that Somalia is dangerous. Any other place you're interested in going to? Any place you haven't been?"

She shrugged. "Well…I haven't been to Ibiza but have a trip planned there for this summer. I did go to Madrid last summer."

He laughed. "Everyone goes there to vacation. That hardly sounds daring."

"I went to see a bullfight," she said.

"What did you like about it?"

"The pageantry, the excitement. We did a cover story about six months ago…actually it will be on the stands this month. It was about two brothers who were matadors— fifth-generation matadors. These men are rock stars in Spain.

"Does that sound ridiculous?" she asked.

"Not at all. It makes you sound like a very interesting woman. A woman whom I'm very glad to have gotten to know a little better tonight. How long have you been in the UK?" he asked.

"Almost three years," she said.

"Why did you come here?" he asked.

She struggled now. Outright lying to him might come back to bite her later, but that previous encounter had scared her and shaped her into the woman she was today and she couldn't regret that.

"For my job."

"That's pretty daring," he said. "Leaving behind your home and your family to come to another country."

The way he said it made her feel special. As if she were unique to him. And looking into his dark eyes she felt like he was seeing her. Not just her body or her position at the magazine. The fact that Steven liked her for herself—that seduced her more than anything else.

Five

Steven leaned forward and kissed her. It was a soft kiss that felt like it went on for days. He didn't touch her anywhere but where their mouths met. She felt as if they had all the time in the world, that there were only the two of them and this moment, which would never end.

She kept her eyes open at first because she wanted to see him. His eyes were closed and she felt the intensity in him. But this time it was focused all on her. She closed her own eyes because she didn't want to see his vulnerability. But even as she did so, she couldn't help but feel her heart melt a little. No matter how intense or driven Steven seemed, he still had some vulnerabilities.

Soon she didn't think about anything but the kiss. The way his mouth felt against hers. The taste of him, which was just right. She wanted to experience everything she could of Steven. She wanted to know so much more than the taste of his mouth on hers. She wanted to feel his hands around her waist again. To have him pull her closer.

He lifted his head up and she took a moment to compose herself before she opened her eyes. She didn't want to be any more vulnerable to him than she already was and she certainly didn't want him to glimpse her vulnerability.

She rested her head against the wall and opened her eyes. He was staring down at her, those hawklike eyes assessing her.

"What are you thinking?" she asked.

"That no other woman has ever tasted as good as you," he said.

She felt overwhelmed by this comment. They were traveling the same path in so many ways. This man— Steven Devonshire—could be more to her than a date... "I was thinking the same thing."

"That I kiss like a woman?" he asked.

She laughed and the intensity of the moment was broken. She knew it was for the best because it showed her exactly where Steven was in his thinking. And it kept her from thinking that this was more than it was.

They'd had dinner and now he was trying to score. At the end of the day she had to remember that this was Steven Devonshire, the man who'd left her in ruins. He was more dangerous to her than a seven-layer chocolate cake, because she could exercise off the effects of a choco-binge but she couldn't fix her battered emotions nearly as easily.

"Still want that drink?" she asked, not sure she wanted him to stay.

He shook his head. "I think I should be going."

She did, too. She ducked out from under his arms. She opened her front door, leaning back against it. The chill of the night air swept into her warm little house.

She shivered as she waited for Steven to leave. He turned and crossed the threshold. His car was parked at the curb, in front of her very old and very temperamental MG. But she loved that car despite its problems.

"Will you have dinner with me again?" he asked.

"Yes," she said. "But I'm flying to New York tomorrow for a meeting with the team for our American magazine."

"How long will you be gone?"

"Four days," she said. "But I won't be able to function until six days. Jet lag slows me down."

"Then we'll have dinner six days from now…that's next Monday. I'll pick you up here at home."

Ainsley realized that Steven was used to giving orders. "Do people always do what you say?"

"Most times," he admitted.

"You can pick me up at my office. I'm not going to be home in time for a dinner date."

"Very well. My assistant will call your office tomorrow to get all your contact information—e-mail address and so on. That way I can be in touch with you when you're in the States."

"What would you need to talk to me about?"

"The story, of course," he said.

"I have assigned a writer to the story and my boss wants the U.S. magazine to run the article as well. So we might actually have two writers working on this."

"Sounds good to me," he said.

She stood there until he got in his car and drove away. She stepped inside and closed the door, fastened the lock and leaned back against the door.

Steven Devonshire had kissed her.

She shouldn't put too much emphasis on it. It was

nothing more than a kiss from a man. A man she found interesting...oh, heck, who was she kidding? Steven had been the man that she'd been obsessed with for five long years.

After his comment and the massively embarrassing debacle at the *Business Journal,* she'd had no choice but to start over—and she had. Now she was focused on work and on herself. And her little habit of following Steven—almost cyber stalking him—had to stop. She'd kept tabs on him, hoping that someday their paths would cross again and she'd come out the victor. But tonight had shown her that she still had weaknesses as far as he was concerned.

No matter how much she'd read about him, she was just starting to realize that she didn't know everything about the man. The stuff she'd read barely scratched the surface of him. Words like *intense* conjured an image of a certain kind of man and Steven was so much more in real life.

And he'd kissed her.

"Stop building dreams," she warned herself. She walked through her house, kicking off her heels as she went along. Her mother hated that habit, but Ainsley always left a trail of shoes near her front door.

In her tiny kitchen, she opened her liquor cabinet, poured herself a splash of cognac and drank it. This was nothing.

She had her career and it was on track. She wasn't about to let Steven derail her. It would be so easy to just give in to her own desires and start thinking in terms of a real relationship with him, but she couldn't forget that behind that charming facade he was a pit bull.

Later on as she lay in her own bed staring at the ceiling, sleep eluded her. Instead, all she could think about was that she should have taken his hand and led him back to her bed. She should never have let him walk out her front door. Because she knew tomorrow she was going to start doubting that a man as handsome and sexy as Steven Devonshire could really want a girl like her.

Two days later Steven found himself in an odd predicament. He was in the middle of a meeting with the Everest Mega Store team at the Leicester Square location when he caught a glimpse of a woman on the retail floor who looked like Ainsley. He knew Ainsley was in New York and it couldn't be her, but he watched the woman for a minute just to make sure it wasn't her.

She was an obsession for him. He should have bedded her the first night they were together. Instead, he had waited because he wanted to unravel her secrets. Now he was thinking, secrets be damned. He wanted her out of his mind so he could get back to normal.

He wasn't the type of man to spend too much time thinking about a woman—any woman. But with Ainsley on his mind all the time he was starting to believe that something dangerous was happening to him.

"Mr. Devonshire?"

His secretary stood in the doorway. The woman was proving to be a good fit here.

"There is a woman downstairs asking for you," Marta said.

Was it Ainsley? He would be very surprised if it was. But if this attraction he felt was two-way, maybe she had come back early.

"Did she give a name?"

"Dinah...I can't recall her last name, sir."

Dinah. That was what came of letting a woman

preoccupy his mind. "I'll be downstairs and then back at the office. Can you finish up here, Marta?"

"Yes, sir."

"Take your lunch and then be back by two."

He walked out of the office. Dinah, his executive vice president, waited in the middle of the retail floor where a display of classic 1970s musicians was displayed. There was a full-sized cardboard cutout of Tiffany Malone—Henry's mother.

An earthy sexuality suffused her stare. Her hair was tousled and she wore a pair of skintight, faded denim jeans and a flowing top. It was a classic seventies photo, but Henry's mother made it so much more. She looked iconic standing there.

He wondered how Malcolm could have been attracted to his mother after being with someone so overtly sexual. His mum exuded none of that. She was smart and classically beautiful, but compared to Tiffany Malone...she would definitely come in second.

"Thanks for getting here so quickly," he said to Dinah.

"Not a problem. You promised me a nice bonus, so I wanted to jump in and get started on this project of yours," she said.

"Just the attitude I like. Let's discuss the details back at my office."

"Okay, but why did you have me meet you here?" she asked.

"I want you to take a look around. This is our best-performing store. What are they doing here that is different?"

"You want me to go to all the stores?"

"Not all of them, but most of them. I want to know

if it's the location or if it's the product. Should we have something different in each location? I mean in addition to the music."

"Very well," Dinah said. They walked the store. He and Dinah made notes on what they saw and then they went back to the office to discuss their findings.

Steven stayed late at the office and worked. It hadn't taken him too long to realize he could easily beat both of his half brothers in this competition. He'd had the financials from the record label and the airline sent to his office. Dinah had e-mailed her recommendations for the North American operation based on the data they had.

Someone should go to New York, he thought. They needed to see the operation there to make sure that their recommendations could be implemented.

He picked up the phone and dialed Dinah's number.

"Yes, boss?"

"How do you feel about a trip to New York?"

"Like you are a mind reader. I was composing an e-mail to that effect when you called. I'd like to take Harry from finance with me."

They discussed the details of her trip and he thought of Ainsley in Manhattan. Steven was pleased with Dinah's plan of-action. She'd check in daily, but he didn't like to micromanage unless things were going poorly. He hired the best people so he didn't have to do their jobs for him.

It was midnight when he was ready to leave the office. And he took a moment to log in to his personal e-mail account. He wanted Ainsley. And he wanted her to be thinking of him.

He wanted to disturb her workday the way she had his. Because although he'd been focused on work, she'd been like a shadow in his mind making him wonder what her day was like. It was five in the morning in Manhattan and he wanted her first thought to be of him and their date.

He composed an e-mail to her. Taking his time with his words because he wanted every moment between now and the time they were face-to-face again to be a slow seduction.

I can't stop thinking about you. The feel of your lips under mine and the scent of your perfume lingers in the air around me. Be safe in New York.
Steven

He could have written more, but he preferred to be subtle. He'd learned early in life that small gestures often had a deeper impact that big, flashy ones.

He hit Send and left the office. The streets in the financial district weren't busy and he made his way easily though the traffic, which was a good thing because he found himself thinking of Ainsley next to him in his car.

The scent of her perfume hung in the air; it was almost as if she were there. He shook his head, hoping to dislodge the thoughts of her and find his peace again.

Once he got home and undressed, he lay naked in his king-size bed and groaned. He remembered the feel of her curvy body against his and the taste of her mouth under his.

Ainsley had a hard time adjusting to the time change. She'd gone to bed at six p.m. yesterday and gotten up at five. She had a lot of meetings to attend and would be getting as much work done as possible.

Freddie had accompanied her, since he was her right-hand man. They had always worked together as a team, and even though she was the boss that relationship—the closeness of it—had remained.

He kept odd hours, though, and she doubted he'd be awake now. So she called room service and ordered a pot of coffee and fiber cereal and fruit for breakfast. She wanted to order the New York cheesecake with strawberry sauce and in the old days she would have, but she forced out the word *muesli* and hung up before she could give in and order something fattening.

It was silly, but she was constantly battling with food. She had talked to her leader about it when she'd been on Weight Watchers full time and Marianne had suggested that she used food to cope with life.

Ainsley knew that was true. She'd been overweight most of her life and then at college, when she'd been on her own, she'd found comfort in doughnuts and carbs. Before she knew it, she was obese. That had helped with her studies. Had made it so much easier to focus on her education because most men weren't in the least bit interested in her.

It had been almost three months since she'd been tempted by a sweet like the cheesecake. And she knew that it was because of Steven.

He was making her feel unsure of herself, and she had always combated those feelings with food. It didn't help matters that she knew if she were fat he probably wouldn't have even noticed her. Ugh, this was making her crazy—*he* was making her crazy.

When she closed her eyes, she could still see his face as he'd kissed her. And she wanted to be a girl worthy of his attention. She wanted him not to be disappointed in her. But she was afraid that wouldn't be the case.

She had lost all her weight by dieting, not by exercising. So even though she was slim now, she still had parts that weren't as fit and toned as those of someone who hit the gym every day, twice a day.

What if he saw her naked and changed his mind about her? What if...

She'd never been this wishy-washy. Any other man she would just walk away from. But this was Steven. The man she'd always wanted.

She wasn't going to let her doubts feed her food obsession. She wasn't going to let her doubts overwhelm her or let her miss the opportunity to be with him. She wasn't going to let her doubts control her. If she'd done that, she'd still be sitting in her apartment in Chicago having never left school.

She opened her e-mail to find the very first one was from Steven. She read it and felt herself flush. She needed to be much more confident if she was going to be with him. But she had no idea how to do that. She couldn't change the fears she'd always had of her body that easily.

She walked away from her computer and stood in front of the mirror. She stared at her features. Her face was so different now that she scarcely recognized herself sometimes: her cheekbones thin and prominent, her mouth still full and pouty. The biggest change had been her figure.

No it wasn't, she reminded herself. The biggest change had come at work. She remembered when she'd been called to Maurice Sheffield's office. The owner of the Sheffield Group had taken thirty minutes out of his day to congratulate her on running the *British Fashion Quarterly* and bringing up revenue at the magazine. No one got thirty minutes with Maurice, her boss and the publisher and CEO of the consortium.

She looked at the slim woman in the reflection and wondered where she'd come from and prayed in the same breath that she'd never leave. In her heart she knew that her weight had nothing to do with her success. She'd changed on the inside and she just wished she'd stop seeing the old Ainsley when she looked in the mirror.

She shook her head. She needed to believe in herself as a person the way she believed in herself as a professional. She was capable of winning Steven's affection...was that what she wanted?

Her assistant, Cathy, had sent a note to Tiffany Malone, Lynn Grandings and Princess Louisa to see if they'd consider being interviewed. Maurice loved the idea of a retrospective fashion piece on these women, and Ainsley wasn't about to disappoint her boss.

Freddie had suggested letting Danielle do the interviews, but Ainsley wasn't about to risk giving it to someone she had placed on probation. Instead, she had assigned the story to Bert Michaels. He'd interviewed Prince Harry last year for a Mother's Day piece they'd run about how mothers influence fashion—his mother had set a standard many other women were still trying to live up to.

And she had an appointment with Malcolm's attorney to talk about interviewing him. Malcolm Devonshire was one of the most famous personalities of their time. He was legendary not just for his affairs but also for his zest for life. As much as he lived big, he'd been very private about his personal life. Only the tabloids had ever run stories about him.

If she got an interview with him in her magazine she'd

have landed a real coup. Something that her bosses wouldn't overlook. And it wasn't lost on Ainsley that meeting Steven that day in the Everest Mega Store had been fortuitous.

She showered and dressed, keeping her mind firmly on her meetings for the day, but before she left her hotel she knew she wanted to return Steven's e-mail. She just had no idea what to say to him.

Somehow *Me, too* didn't seem like the right response. Yet more than that might be making promises that she wasn't sure she could keep. When she was with Steven, it was easy to forget herself. Forget her fears and the fact that she wasn't who he thought she was.

But apart from him she could count the obstacles between them. She had too little experience and he had too much. She was a small-town girl and he was the son of a billionaire and a world-renowned scientist.

But none of that mattered when they were together. Nothing mattered except the way his hands felt on her. The way his taste lingered on her lips after he'd kissed her. The way the scent of his cologne lingered after he left.

He was just so much more than she thought he would be. And there were still so many questions she had about him. So many answers that she wasn't sure she'd ever get.

Yet she wasn't going to give up. When she'd decided to change her life and lose weight, she'd made a promise to herself to stop hiding. And she had done a good job of it until now.

Steven was the kind of man she should be going after. But first she had to figure out what to say.

She hit the Reply key on the e-mail and sat down at the chair, trying to be more comfortable.

Dear Steven

    No, that sounded too businesslike.

You've haunted my dreams.

    She hit Send before she could change her mind.

Six

Steven decided at the last minute to go to New York himself instead of sending Dinah and he was glad that he had. The Everest Mega Store in Times Square was a major asset, and as he walked the floor with the VP of the North American unit, Hobbs Colby, he realized that Hobbs had some great ideas on ways to capitalize on the store's potential.

"Let's go back to the office and figure out how to make the most of this store," Steven said.

Steven followed Hobbs into the conference room on the third floor. There was a radio broadcast studio built right into the store so they could do live broadcasts and this conference room overlooked the selling floor.

"I think this property is an asset we aren't exploiting to its fullest. I want to set up live broadcasts from here for all Everest recording artists," Steven said. "Let's make this place into the go-to spot for live music promotions. I want release parties and signings."

"That won't be a problem on our end. Typically I've had trouble getting Everest Records to return my calls. I know I'm new, but I worked for a concert promoter for years so I have the experience to do those kinds of events."

"Let me make a few calls. Give me a minute—I'll call right now," Steven said.

Hobbs nodded and left, and Steven got Henry on the line. Though it was about ten at night in London, he knew that Henry would still be up.

"Devonshire," Henry said.

"It's Steven. I'm in New York and I wanted to go over something with you. Can you talk?"

"Certainly. I'm in a club. Give me a minute to find someplace quiet."

Steven held the line.

"Okay, what's up?"

"I'm not sure how familiar you are with our retail stores, but some of them were set up to do live remote broadcasts for radio. This store in Times Square has the facilities not only for that but for live performances as well. My U.S. VP, Hobbs Colby, has been trying to get some artists to come here and perform."

"I haven't had a chance to call him back yet. What are you thinking?" Henry asked.

"That we use this place for exclusive North American releases of our CDs. Maybe one week early? Not sure how you feel about that. Then we need to book the groups into this store. I think this will help both of our business units."

"I agree. Let me talk to the artists and I'll get back to you."

"Thanks, Henry."

Steven spent the rest of the afternoon in meetings and on the phone working on getting the ball rolling. "What other stores do we have with these kinds of facilities?"

"Miami, LA, Vancouver, Toronto, Chicago and Orlando. We can update other facilities if you think that it would be worth our while."

Steven shook his head. "Not yet. Let's do a pilot program at these locations first. I don't want to have the same groups everywhere. I think we should brand each of the locations with a genre. Build up a strong local following. I think New York and LA would be great for any group, but in Miami we should book our Latin groups."

Hobbs nodded. "That works for me. I'll get some ideas to you."

"I'm in New York for two more days. We'll talk more in the morning," Steven said.

Hobbs left and Steven checked the e-mail on his iPhone. That one from Ainsley early this morning was still at the top of his inbox. He'd made the decision to come and see her after reading that she was haunted by him the same way he'd been haunted by her.

He hadn't wanted to wait a week to see her again and he wasn't a man who hesitated when he wanted something. He knew that pursuing Ainsley was complicated. But he didn't let that stand in his way. He'd had to work for everything he had in his life.

His phone rang while he was debating how to contact Ainsley.

"Hello, Aunt Lucy."

"Hello, Steven, how are you today?"

"I'm good. What can I do for you?" he asked.

"Are you available for dinner tomorrow night? I'm coming to London."

"I'm sorry, but I'm out of town right now," he said.

She sighed. "I wish you'd make more time for your family."

"I see you once a month," he said.

He didn't like to think about his childhood. He'd grown up alone and his aunt Lucy had been too busy with her own career as a chef then to notice him—much as his mother had been. But when he'd been a teenager, Steven had gotten into some trouble with drinking and for some reason that had made Lucy notice him.

She'd tried to force a relationship between them, but it had been too little, too late. His character had already become firmly entrenched, and that character wasn't a family guy.

"That's right, you do. You know I'm here if you need me."

"I do. I've got to go now. I'm going into a meeting."

"Goodbye, Steven. I love you."

"Bye, Aunt Lucy." He never said the L-word. He wasn't even sure that emotion existed for him.

Hanging up the phone, he called his assistant and had her find out where Ainsley was staying. He wasn't just here for business, even though he knew he should be focusing his energies on the Everest Mega Stores, he was also very interested in Ainsley Patterson.

It had been a long, exhausting day and when Ainsley got to her hotel in the middle of Times Square she wanted nothing more than to head to bed. But as she walked through the lobby she heard someone call her name. Not just anyone—Steven Devonshire.

"What are you doing here?" she asked.

She didn't want to see Steven here. Here in Manhattan was where she'd had her horrible interview and her career had gone down in flames. She mentally shook herself. She'd started over and she needed to stop thinking of Steven as her own personal Waterloo. She needed to remember that he'd made her into the woman she was today. No, that wasn't right. *She'd* made herself into the woman she was today.

"Is that any way to greet the man who haunts your dreams?"

"I knew I'd regret writing that."

"Is it true?"

"I'm not a liar," she said.

"Good. I'm in town on business and I'm free this evening."

"Aren't you lucky. I am, too," she said. "Would you like to have drinks?"

Since he was here, she decided to take control of this relationship.

"I'd love that. I know a place close by, Blue Fin."

"I need to change and then we can go."

"You look lovely," he said.

She shook her head. "Thank you, but I need a few minutes."

"Not a problem. I'll meet you back here in thirty minutes."

"Okay."

Ainsley left him in the lobby and took the glass elevator up to her suite. She changed into a pair of tight-fitting jeans and a cami top she usually wore under her suit. She undid the ponytail she typically wore at work and fluffed her hair around her shoulders. Then she put on fresh makeup and went back downstairs.

Steven was waiting where she'd left him, but typing on his iPhone when she approached. She gave him some distance to finish in private.

"You look so incredible tonight," he said.

She nodded. His compliment made her uncomfortable.

He put his hand on the small of her back as they walked out of the lobby. The foot traffic was heavy on this early spring evening. Steven kept her close to him and made sure that no one bumped into her as they were walking. They didn't talk until they were seated at a high table in the bar, Bluetinis in each of their hands. "I love the Swedish fish in the bottom," Ainsley said.

"Women always do," Steven said.

That gave her pause. "Have you taken a lot of women here?"

"No. I just meant that women like sweet things. My mum is crazy for wine gums."

Ainsley arched an eyebrow at him. "They are pretty yummy."

"That was my point."

She shook her head. "Why didn't you mention you'd be in New York when I said I was coming here?"

"I wanted to surprise you."

"You did. You are not turning out to be what I expected."

"What did you expect?" he asked, taking a sip of his drink.

"Someone a little colder," she said.

"Why?"

"I'd just heard that you can be kind of callous in business."

"That's business."

"Are you different in your personal relationships?" she asked.

He looked distinctly uncomfortable and leaned toward her to answer. "I—"

"Ainsley! What are you doing out?" Freddie asked as he approached their table. "I thought you were calling it an early evening."

Damn, she wanted to know what Steven would have said in response to her query. "I ran into Steven and we decided to have a drink. Steven, this is Frederick VonHauser. He works for me at *Fashion Quarterly*. Freddie, this is Steven Devonshire."

Freddie gave her a surprised look. "Mind if I join you? I'm meeting some friends, but I'm a little early."

Ainsley started to say no, but Steven nodded and gestured to the chair. "Have a seat."

Freddie sat down between them and Ainsley instantly wished that her friend would leave. She didn't want Freddie and Steven to talk. Didn't want to risk Freddie saying something that would remind Steven of the woman she had been.

"How long are you in town?" Freddie asked.

"Just three days. I have recently taken over the Everest Mega Stores and I'm checking out our North American operation."

"So it's just coincidence that you are here when Ainsley is?"

"Indeed. A happy one," Steven said, looking straight at her.

She knew she shouldn't read too much into that, but she

also realized he'd come to New York to see her and that meant a lot to her.

"Sounds like it," Freddie said. "I see my friends, so I'll leave you two. Enjoy your evening."

"We will," Ainsley said.

"Sorry about that," Steven said after Freddie left. "You seemed a little uncomfortable."

"I just wasn't expecting to see anyone from work."

"Is that an issue?" he asked.

"It might be. I don't want to have the journalistic integrity of the article compromised because we're seeing each other. If we're going to see each other, I need to talk to my boss."

"With the focus of the articles on the mothers of the heirs, I would think that would take care of any conflict of interest," he said.

"Would it matter so much if we didn't see each other again?" she asked. She needed to know. She wasn't about to compromise her career for a man who was simply trying to score.

"Yes, it would. I wasn't playing games with you when I sent that e-mail. I can't stop thinking about you, Ainsley, and that's very dangerous for me because I'm used to being focused only on business."

"Me, too," she admitted.

"Good. We'll figure this out."

She nodded toward him. They finished their drinks and then Steven left for his dinner appointment. She went back to her hotel.

She knew she wanted to see Steven again, and if that was going to happen then she needed to clear it with her boss. She wasn't about to lose another job because of Steven Devonshire.

* * *

The next morning Ainsley woke up to a knock on her door. There was a delivery for her—a huge bouquet of flowers. She carried them to her sitting area and then checked the card. They were from Steven.

In his scrawling handwriting was a simple note that thanked her for the evening and told her he couldn't wait to see her again.

She held the card in her hand and sat down next to the flowers. She didn't want to fall for Steven, but when he did things like this it was hard not to.

All her life she'd been a misfit. She hadn't dated in high school because she'd been a chubby bookworm. And in college she'd just sort of muddled through. She'd had a boyfriend there, but Barry hadn't been the dream lover she'd longed for, and she'd ended up pouring herself into her classes and eventually her job: working and eating and pretending that her job was enough.

But when she'd lost it because of Steven, her awakening had changed her focus, but it hadn't changed her dreams for the future. She'd never pictured herself in a long-term relationship.

She'd always been happy on her own. Now, though, she was dreaming of Steven, wanting to wake up with him—and she didn't even know what that meant. She was scared to think that she was coming to need him. She didn't want to need a man like Steven Devonshire.

She put down the card and picked up her phone. If she were going to take a chance on dating Steven, on letting him be important to her, she had to make sure that Maurice wasn't going to fire her over this.

She dialed his direct line and he answered on the third ring.

"It's Ainsley."

"Good morning, Ainsley. Did you get our Devonshire story details locked up?"

"I'm still working on that, sir. But I did need to talk to you about something."

"Yes?"

"Steven Devonshire asked me out and I'd like to go out with him. I don't want it to affect our story. However, I thought since we are going to run the article in the U.S. and UK editions, it might not be a problem. The focus of the articles is on the mothers and Malcolm."

"Let me think about this, Ainsley. I don't want to stand in the way of your personal life. As far as I know, you rarely do anything but work."

"That's true, sir. This job is my life."

"I can understand that. But having a life is important, too. I think we'll add a note that you are dating Steven if it turns out that you are and since the focus is on fashion I think we'll be okay."

"Thanks, Maurice."

"You're welcome. Now get me all the people I need for this article so it can rock."

"I will."

She hung up and realized that she had no more excuses to keep Steven at bay. She wasn't going to lose her job over him and that was reassuring, but it also took away her safe out if things got too deep, too fast. One part of her was happy about that; the other was a bit worried.

She thought she was still in control of her life. But her heart argued that it would be making the decisions when it came to Steven.

Seven

"How was your date?" Freddie asked as he joined her in the cab at the end of their third day in New York.

"What date?"

"With Steven Devonshire. We haven't had a moment to chat and I want all the details. Was it everything you thought it would be? Did birds sing? The heavens open up?"

She punched him playfully in the arm. "You make me sound like...someone who is obsessed. It was just drinks. He's a very sophisticated and charming man."

"What makes him sophisticated?"

"His choices."

"Tell me everything."

She wanted to laugh at the way he said it, but she knew that she'd never share what she felt about Steven with Freddie. It was one thing to let him know about what she'd read on the Internet, but how Steven kissed was personal and she wasn't about to share it.

"It was just a nice evening."

"A nice evening? What are you hiding? Do you like him?"

She shook her head. "It's complicated."

She wanted the taxi ride to be over. But of course it was rush hour and they'd be stuck here for at least thirty minutes. *Damn.*

"Tell me."

"I can't. I haven't figured it out yet myself," she said.

He reached over and patted her knee. "I'm here if you want to talk."

"Thanks," she said. "Isn't it funny how foreign this city feels?"

He laughed. "Yes. I think we've been in London too long."

"It's only been three years. Do you ever think of coming back?" she asked him.

"Never. I like London. And my best friend lives there."

She smiled at him and blew him an air kiss. "We'd still be BFFs if you moved."

"You say that, but life would change. Besides, I have my Maxim now and he likes our quiet neighborhood."

Maxim was Freddie's English Bulldog. And she knew he'd never move if he thought that dog would be traumatized by it. He was so attached to him that he'd set up a webcam so he could chat with the dog once a day while he was on this trip.

She made small talk until traffic started moving. Her BlackBerry pinged and she glanced down at her e-mail—she didn't know how she'd live without her BlackBerry—and saw that Tiffany Malone had accepted the invitation to do an interview.

"Yes! Just what I was hoping for. Tiffany Malone said yes to the interview."

"She's one of my faves. Her music was so earthy. It's a shame she stopped performing."

Ainsley nodded and typed an e-mail back to her assistant to finalize the details for the interview. She would use the leverage of Tiffany's agreement to secure an interview with the other women. No one had ever printed their stories and it was past time that those women had a voice.

She sent a personal note to Tiffany, telling her that one of their writers—Bert Michaels—would be in touch with her soon. Once the article was written they'd compile pictures from the past and present to round out the piece.

The rest of the day was busy, but Maurice wanted her to lock in all three of the Devonshire heirs for the interview. Cathy had tried, but her secretary hadn't been able to get the men to return her calls, so Ainsley knew she'd have to do it herself. Geoff was difficult to reach, so she had to settle for leaving a voice mail.

She called Henry's office and got his assistant, Astrid, who put her right through.

"Hello, Henry. This is Ainsley Patterson with *Fashion Quarterly*. I spoke to Steven a few days ago and he intimated that you'd be agreeable to participating in an interview with our magazine."

"I can't say no. My mum would have my head. She told me you were going to interview her."

"We are. Once I have a confirmation from Geoff, my assistant will call you and set up the times and all that. I'd love to photograph you with your mother and maybe get one with all three of you boys and Malcolm."

"Good luck with that. I'm not sure that Malcolm's health will allow it."

"If it does, will you participate?"

"I'll think about it. Probably."

"Thank you, Henry."

"No problem. According to my mum, your magazine is one of the best. She had nothing but great things to say about it."

"Thanks," she said. She ended the call a few minutes later and then dialed Steven's number.

He answered it on the third ring. "Devonshire."

"It's Ainsley." She didn't want to mention last night or the fact that they were both in New York.

"What can I do for you?"

"I need you to talk to your mother about the interview. Tiffany Malone has already agreed. If we can get your mum as well it would be a more well-rounded interview."

"I was hoping you were calling to talk about our date."

"Nope."

"That's a very American answer."

"Is it? I can't talk about that right now. I'm in a conference room with other staff members."

"So you're not alone?"

"Exactly."

"If I talk dirty to you will you blush?" he asked, his voice deepening.

"Probably," she admitted.

"I will do my best to get my mum to agree, but someone is going to have to go to Berne to interview her. Her work is entering a critical stage and I know she won't leave."

"Should I go there and ask her?"

"It might help."

"Okay. I'll work that out. I guess that's all for now."

"I suppose that is. I can't wait to kiss you again," he said.

"Me, too," she said, preparing to disconnect before he could say anything else.

"Are you available for dinner tonight?" he asked.

"No. I think we'll have to wait until we're back in London," she said.

He agreed and hung up. She thought that she'd dodged a bullet. She was cool and confident when it came to business, but the personal aspect of her relationship with Steven scared her.

Steven left a message for his mother with Roman, his mother's lab partner and assistant, to alert her that Ainsley would be calling. Roman had been working with Lynn for the last fifteen years. Steven actually liked the man; he was funny.

"How are you, Steven? Your mum mentioned that you were running Malcolm's business now."

She would put it that way. Either she didn't listen to what he'd said or she simply assumed that he'd won the competition that Malcolm had set up for all his heirs.

"It's going well. I'm not running the show yet, but I've been here less than a week."

Roman laughed. "I'll give you one more week to get everything in order."

"That should just about do it. Will you let my mum know I need to speak to her?"

"Of course I will. She's spending most of her nights in the lab, so if you try after nine, you can probably reach her there."

"Thanks," Steven said. Thinking back he realized

that he'd always learned what his mother was doing from Roman. It had been that way his entire life.

"I'll call back later."

Steven had a lot of information to go through and he spent the rest of the day running numbers. He was happy when Geoff called and invited him to join him for dinner.

Steven often wondered if his life would have been different had he and Geoff met when they were boys. Steven had used Malcolm's name to gain entrance to Eton. The prestigious school the young princes had attended was extremely hard to get into. And Geoff's mother's family had been going there for generations. But at the last moment Geoff had been sent to a school in the States.

Steven had always believed it was because of the publicity that had surrounded the enrollment of two of the Devonshire bastards. That had been the first time that he had become aware of how many people were interested in the circumstances of his birth.

It had been a bit overwhelming—he'd almost asked his mother to withdraw him, but she'd been called to a meeting in Switzerland and he'd had no choice but to go to school as scheduled.

He shook his head. He had forgotten what it had been like to be that boy. He'd been scared and had felt out of place there. He wasn't a boy with the family background of the other boys who attended Eton. And he had quickly learned to fend for himself. He'd used his wits to survive and that had been his first lesson in how to succeed in this life.

Geoff was waiting at the club when he got there. It didn't surprise him. Geoff had struck him as someone who didn't like to keep others waiting.

"Thanks for agreeing to meet me."

"No problem. What's up?"

"I wanted to talk to you about the interviews that you agreed we'd do with *Fashion Quarterly*."

"Of course. What's the problem?"

"My mum doesn't really like publicity and the editor-in-chief has called her a couple of times. She has never talked about her affair with Malcolm and she moved on when she married my stepfather…she just doesn't want to discuss the past."

"I understand that. I have no idea if my mum will agree to the interviews or not. I do know that Tiffany Malone agreed to do it. So she will be sharing her perspective on what happened."

Geoff took a long swallow of his drink. "I don't know what to do. I think that having just Tiffany's story will be a bit odd. Will they still do the interview with us?"

Steven had no idea. He suspected that Ainsley would. She wanted to talk to them. "Probably. She wants to talk to Malcolm, too."

"I wish her success with that, but he wasn't much for agreeing to things when he was healthy. I can't see him doing it now."

Steven would have concurred, except he'd seen Ainsley in action and he was willing to bet that if she got in to see Malcolm, she'd find a way to convince him to do it. She'd find an angle that he wouldn't be able to say no to.

"I'm going to try to convince my mum to do the interview. I want to hear her side of the entire affair," Steven said.

Geoff shrugged. "My mum will be harder to convince, but I'll bet if she hears that Tiffany and Lynn are doing it she'll agree as well. Of course, she'll have to coordinate with the royal family's PR department."

"I hope so. Ainsley is really hot to do this interview and I've been working the business angle. I know she wants to talk about the past, but I want each of us to talk about the new things happening in each business unit."

"Henry and I are collaborating by painting the album covers of his new artists on the side of several of our planes."

"I love that idea," Steven said. "I think we'll produce some T-shirts picturing the album covers to sell in the store. And maybe we can run a promo the first week the CD comes out to bundle the shirts with the CD."

"Yes, that'll work. I'm sure Henry will agree to it," Geoff said.

They talked more about the business and it wasn't lost on Steven that the father he'd never known had given him brothers that he had a lot in common with. As a man who'd always been on his own, it was unnerving to realize that he finally had a family.

More than his mum and Aunt Lucy anyway. He wasn't sure he liked it. But he did know that Henry and Geoff were men he'd have hired to work for him. They were driven and innovative and together the three of them were going to take the Everest Group to heights that Malcolm had only dreamed of.

Ainsley's office overlooked the Basilica at St. Peter's Cathedral. She stood at the window as dusk fell over the city and thought about the coming evening. New York had been exhausting and she'd spent too much time in the offices there. She was glad to be back home.

She wasn't sure when it had happened, but at some point

in the last three years London had become home. She'd gotten used to the sights and sounds of this city and made it her own.

Her assistant, Cathy, stood in the doorway when Ainsley turned around. "I thought you'd left."

"Not yet. I had something that I wanted to talk to you about. Geoff Devonshire wants to meet with you before he will agree to be a part of the interviews."

Ainsley thought that Steven had already gotten the approval of his half brothers so this was news to her. "Fine. When is he available?"

"Um…he's actually in the reception area. He stopped by and wouldn't take no for an answer."

Cathy guarded her office like a shark, so to hear that Geoff had somehow gotten her to put him in the reception area surprised her.

"He's charming?"

"And so very handsome," she said. "Too handsome. But I also knew you wanted this locked up so I figured I'd let him stay."

"Good thinking. Hiring you was a very smart decision," Ainsley said.

"As I remind you daily," Cathy said, turning toward the door. "I'll go get him. Do you want me to interrupt after ten minutes?"

Ainsley rarely had time in her schedule to give anyone more than ten minutes, and from the beginning she and Cathy had an agreement that the assistant would come in and stop the meeting if it ran long.

She had dinner reservations with Steven tonight. Would there be time to collect herself before he arrived?

"Yes, please."

"Okay. I have put some things for your signature in your

box. If you want to be efficient and sign them now, I can process them while you're in your meeting."

"You're getting a little too bossy, Cath."

"That's the only way I keep you in line," she said, walking out the door with a smile.

Ainsley reached for the folder that Cathy had mentioned. Inside were some mock-ups for the cover of their current issue. She made notes on three of them. None of them were that exciting. She was going to have to address this first thing in the morning at their staff meeting. She made a note for Cathy to make sure that those responsible for the cover shoot were there.

Then she moved on to the photos Davis Montgomery had taken of Jon BonGiovanni. They were perfect. She approved three of them for use before she heard her door open.

She stood up to greet Geoff Devonshire. He looked tall and elegant and, aside from the set of his eyes and his jaw, he scarcely resembled Steven.

"Hello, Mr. Devonshire. May I call you Geoff?"

"Of course," he said, taking the hand she'd extended for him to shake.

"I'm Ainsley," she said. "Please have a seat. Can I offer you something to drink?"

"I'm good," he said.

"That's all for now, Cathy," Ainsley said to her assistant, handing her the file she'd made notes in.

She walked around her office and sat behind her desk. Sinking down in the big leather chair, she took a moment to make sure he realized that she was in a position of power. That was the only way she dealt with men, she thought. That was why Steven was throwing her. He didn't see just the woman and the job—he saw the woman behind it.

"What can I do for you?" she asked.

"My family is highly private and I agree with Steven that these interviews will be great for our new careers running the Everest Group. However, I have concerns about the questions that you may ask."

She understood that. Geoff was a double-whammy publicity draw. He was a minor member of the current royal family and he was a bastard son of one of the most controversial men in the UK.

"We can draft a list of topics that are off-limits and the writer will not ask about them. If he does, then you can simply decline to answer," she said.

"That's all well and good. But I'm also going to need to approve the final draft of the article."

"I'm not in the habit of doing that, Geoff. Our articles are about the people behind their celebrity."

"I realize that, but this is a deal-breaker for me. I'll give you enough personal information to make the article interesting."

Ainsley wasn't sure he would. But from her dealings with Steven she recognized that stubborn Devonshire will when she came up against it. "You drive a hard bargain."

He smiled at her and when he did he was a breathtakingly handsome man. "So I've been told. But you must understand, my mother is adamant that she will not talk about Malcolm or the circumstances of my birth."

She'd been afraid of that. She had found no recent mention of Princess Louisa in any of the Internet databases she'd searched. The woman was a recluse and had been since the birth of Geoff. Before that she'd been a party girl and the toast of London. "I'd really like to have her in the article. We will do everything to accommodate her and keep her out of the spotlight if that's your desire."

"Yes, it is. But more than that she doesn't want to be profiled in an article with the other mistresses of Malcolm. She had enough of that when I was born. She might agree to a sidebar featuring her. I realize your magazine will probably put the articles in the same issue, but she won't do a photo shoot with the other women."

Ainsley hadn't realized how invasive her idea for the article was to those three women. How had three smart, sexy women all fallen for a man who had kept them all on a string? Her readers would eat up the answer to that question. But how would Geoff, Henry and Steven deal with seeing their mothers back in the spotlight again? That was something she'd have to figure out.

"We will be careful to keep the article within the parameters you mentioned," Ainsley said. She wasn't going to agree to not talking about the past—that made the story juicy.

"That's all I can ask for. The same circumstances apply to her interview—she'll have to approve the questions and such if she grants it. I will submit topics that are off-limits and I will approve the final draft."

Since she had no choice, Ainsley agreed. A few minutes later Geoff left. Cathy was already gone when she changed clothes in her executive bathroom and went downstairs to meet Steven.

Would reading the interview with Steven's mother give her any insight into his character and personality? She wondered if a part of her hadn't come up with this idea because she wanted to know more about the man who'd affected her so deeply. The man who'd changed her. She wanted to know what had shaped him, and the best way to do that would be to talk to his mother.

Though it had only been five days since she'd last seen

him, it seemed much longer when she stepped off the
elevator and saw him waiting in the lobby. He put his hand
on her shoulder and she looked up at him. Saw in his eyes
a hint that maybe he'd missed her, too.

Eight

Ainsley looked as ravishing as he remembered. It ticked him off a little that the attraction he'd felt for her hadn't waned.

While he'd been away from her, he'd speculated that the attraction was driven by lust and had been intensified by his own lack of a current lover. But the moment she'd stepped out of her building he'd known that that was a lie.

"Good evening," he said.

"Hello. How have you been?" she asked. The words were banal, and he who had no patience for small talk wanted it to continue so he could keep listening to her voice.

"Good. I have a bit of a surprise for you," he said. He'd debated taking her to St. Peter's and the upper galleries. It was a beautiful and quiet destination. And it was someplace different.

There was majesty to the cathedral that was unrivaled by anything else in the world, in his opinion. Though it was late, he'd made special arrangements for them to tour the gallery by themselves.

She arched her eyebrow at him and then said, "I love surprises."

"No, you don't," he said. "I've been around you long enough to know that you like to know every detail and you like to be in charge."

"Touché! I think the same could be said of you."

"I've heard it many times. But I think you'll like this surprise."

She didn't say anything else. He held her hand, sliding their fingers together until their palms met. Then he led her out the door of her building and down the street toward St. Peter's. She wore a pair of two-inch, round-toed, patent leather shoes. So she reached his shoulder as they walked. Her thick black hair had been left down and brushed her shoulder with each step she took.

The formfitting black blouse with red decorative buttons accentuated the curves of her breasts. She had the blouse tucked into a long red skirt that ended at her calves. The skirt had a slit on the side that gave him a glimpse of her left leg with each step she took.

He wanted to draw her into a dark alley and have his way with her. Needed to taste those full lips under his. Needed to feel her curvy body pulled flush against his hard angles. Needed…her.

And he needed no one.

"About the interviews," he said, thinking it was time to get all that out of the way.

"Yes, about the interviews. Why didn't you tell me that Geoff was reluctant to be interviewed?"

"I didn't know myself until I spoke to him. But we discussed it and he'll do it."

"I know. He was in my office today. His mother might not be a part of it, which is disappointing."

"I'm sure you'll still have a fabulous story without her. Princess Louisa just doesn't like to speak in public." Ainsley nodded. Steven had never met any of the mothers of the other Devonshire bastards and he'd been curious about that when he'd been younger. But now he knew who he was and what he was trying to accomplish. The past could stay in the past as far as he was concerned.

Ainsley would play a key role in spreading the word to many people that the Everest Group was back. That Everest was the exciting company it used to be and that Everest was about to change the way the world looked at retail marketing.

He wasn't the least bit bothered by the fact that he wanted her and that their business arrangement might be affected by his desires. As they entered St. Peter's and walked up the steps, he was aware that he'd do anything to keep Ainsley by his side. And he wondered just for a moment if he'd suggested the interviews, a gross invasion of his privacy, just to stay by her side.

"St. Peter's?"

"Yes. I have arranged a private tour of the upper galleries."

"Really? I've been dying to see them, but haven't had a chance. Thank you, Steven."

She hugged him and started to pull away quickly, but he brought his hands to her waist and held her there. This was what he'd been waiting for. This was what he wanted. He needed this woman in his arms.

He thought he'd wanted to unravel her mysteries but now

he knew he just wanted her. He didn't care if he unlocked the secrets she kept unless they were secrets about what she hoped he'd do to her.

She wrapped her arms around his neck and tipped her head back to look up at him. Their gazes met and he couldn't help but feel something pass between them. Something hard to define.

"Why haven't you kissed me yet?" she asked.

He didn't answer her, just brought his head down and took her lower lip between his teeth.

Her hands tightened on his shoulders as she tried to pull herself closer to him. This was why he'd waited to kiss her. They were like flint and steel when they touched, and the sparks of the flames they generated consumed both of them.

If he wasn't careful, he'd end up taking Ainsley for the first time in some very public place. And he'd never been much for exhibitionism. She went to his head faster than his first sip of whiskey had and the results were unpredictable.

Tugging her off balance, he pulled her close and felt her settle against him—first her breasts to his chest, then her belly against his stomach. Then she canted her hips toward him so her feminine mound rested against his erection.

He cupped her bottom and held her there while he continued to thrust his tongue deep into her mouth. The sun set around the city and a cold, damp chill filled the air, but he wasn't aware of anything but the woman in his arms.

Ainsley thought of nothing but that kiss for the rest of the evening. As they walked past the crypts of monarchs and poets and through the whispering gallery, all she could think of was Steven and how much she wanted to be alone with him. He had dialed back his attraction and seemed absorbed in what the guide was saying. She tried to listen, but she couldn't help but remember the way his arms had felt against her.

The feeling of the firm grip of his hands on her waist lingered. She could taste him each time she licked her lips.

"Ainsley?"

"Hmm?"

"I was telling our guide how much we enjoyed our tour."

She'd been standing there staring at Steven with a dazed expression. "Yes, we did. Thank you so much."

Steven tipped the man and they left. It was cold outside now that night had fallen and she felt the chill settle over her. She'd left her raincoat at the office. "I forgot my coat."

"I noticed. I thought you were a hardy American."

"I am."

She didn't want him to know that he'd distracted her. While getting all the Devonshire heirs and their mothers to agree to be interviewed was a coup, she normally wouldn't have been involved in the details of a story like this. She would have delegated it. But with Maurice's interest in the story, she was reluctant to let any detail out of her hands. She wanted to be the one to make all the arrangements particularly so she would have an excuse to see Steven.

He shrugged out of his suit jacket and handed it to her. She reached for it, but he drew it out of her grasp.

"Let me help you," he said.

She did, turning to face away from him as he held his jacket up. She slipped her arms inside and was immediately surrounded by his body heat and the scent of aftershave. It was a warm and welcoming feeling, and she was unnerved because as she turned back to Steven, he seemed to know how she felt.

He took her hand in his and continued leading them back toward her office building. His car was still parked on the street and he opened the door for her to get in. "Ready for dinner?"

"Yes," she said. The feelings she had for him were starting to overwhelm her. She wanted to be alone with him. To take off his clothes and see his naked body. But she was also very afraid of that moment. Afraid he'd see past the shields she'd put in place to make the world think she was different from who she really was. Afraid that he would see her naked and turn away from her.

Then she worried that she was worrying for nothing. That he might not even want to make love to her. Her fingers were tightly knotted together, something she realized only as Steven put his hand over hers.

"Relax," he said. "What are you thinking about?"

She couldn't tell him. Couldn't tell this man who exuded sexuality that she was afraid of her own. But then she looked into his dark eyes and remembered the way he'd looked as he'd kissed her that very first time.

She could trust Steven. "I'm not sure I'm like the women you're used to."

"In what way?"

"I haven't had many lovers," she said.

"And that bothers you?"

She shrugged. "Not really. But I think it would be nice to have more experience, especially since you seem to."

He smiled at her, reaching over to stroke her face. "Don't

worry about any of that. You and I are in sync when it comes to physical desire."

"Are you sure? I'm not what you think I am," she said.

He arched one eyebrow at her. "Unless you're secretly a man, I think you are exactly what I believe you to be."

She gave a nervous laugh. "No, I'm not a man."

"Then we have no problem, do we?"

She had wanted to be smooth and confident, but instead she was showing him exactly how vulnerable she was. A part of her knew that letting him see the weakness in her gave him an advantage. She'd heard that the power in a relationship went to the person who wanted the other one less. And she knew that if that were true, she was the one with less power.

She wanted Steven in a way that was overwhelming. It made her do things she'd never done before. She was on a date on a worknight, but then the last time they'd gone out it had been a worknight, too. She always got a good night's sleep so she was sharp at work the next day. She still had e-mails to answer tonight and photos to approve for tomorrow.

But as she sat across from him in a very posh restaurant run by a celebrity chef, she didn't care. She just sat and talked about books and movies, surprised to find that Steven and she had a lot in common.

"Why are you looking at me like that?" she asked toward the end of the meal when he was staring at her mouth.

"I'm wondering how your mouth will feel against my chest," he said. "Will you kiss me there?"

"Yes," she said. The passion and the tension underlying that question brought back all her fears. A surge of electricity cascaded through her. She leaned closer to him at the table. She wanted this man and nothing, not even her own fears, was going to stop her from having him.

She thought he'd ask for the check so they could leave, but instead he took her hand in his under the table and placed it on his thigh. She felt the muscled hardness of his legs and let her fingers caress him.

Steven took a sip of his espresso and kept his hands off Ainsley. It was a struggle because she kept moving her fingers up and down his thigh. He'd taken a gamble by putting her hand there. But her earlier fears had told him that she wasn't sure of her appeal.

And he wondered how a woman as sexy and smart as Ainsley could doubt herself. She had declined dessert, but he'd never known a woman not to want sweets, so he had ordered a seven-layer chocolate cake for them both and offered her a bite.

She shook her head, but he kept the fork extended. "Please take it away, Steven."

He took the bite for himself. "Why?"

Pulling her hand from his leg, she wrapped it around her own waist. "I...I guess this is a good time to tell you. I used to be fat."

Women were always obsessing over five or ten pounds. But Ainsley was perfect. Beautiful, curvy, everything a woman should be.

"I find that very hard to believe."

"Well, it's the truth. Men rarely noticed me when I was in a room."

Again he didn't believe her. "Maybe that was your perception, but I promise you they did."

"No, they didn't."

"Well, then they were fools because I would never have forgotten you," he said.

"But you did," she said. "I interviewed you five years ago. And you don't even remember me."

Steven tried to recall...the girl with the pretty violet eyes? She had been big, he remembered, but more than that she'd been almost invisible when she hadn't been interviewing him. "I remember now. Weren't you A.J. then? You were so shy when the interview was over. Almost as if you wanted to fade into the background."

She flushed. "I did. But you didn't remember me, did you?"

"Not because of the size of your body," he said. "Because you made yourself unremarkable. You've changed. I don't think it's just weight loss. I think it has to do with your personality."

She took a sip of her espresso and then joined her hands together on the table. "A man *would* see it that way."

"Anyone would," he argued. "You used to make yourself invisible. Maybe you felt more comfortable that way. But the woman you are right now is who I'm attracted to, and it wouldn't matter what size she was."

He saw her blink and turn away. "Now I want you to try a bite of this dessert. It's delicious."

"I can't, Steven. One bite will turn into the entire cake. You have no idea what a struggle it is for me to keep from overeating."

She was too disciplined now to overeat. He could tell by the way she held herself that she wouldn't let her control slip. She just wasn't that sure of herself. He vowed that she would be. That he would show her that she was so much more than unfulfilled wanting.

"Trust me."

She looked over at him and he felt like this had become about something more than dessert. The moment sharpened until he knew this would change the course of their relationship. Either she would trust him and it would move forward or she wouldn't and he'd sleep with her and they'd never see each other again.

He wasn't sure which scenario he preferred. Because if she started to trust him, that meant he had the burden of continuing to be worthy of her trust—something he wasn't sure he could do. He'd been dead inside for so long. He'd settled for one-night stands and short-term affairs.

But as the fork was suspended between them and he watched Ainsley move slowly toward it, he knew that things were changing. Not just for her, but for him as well.

She was the first woman he'd wanted physically who had tempted him emotionally. And that scared him. He'd always been alone and he didn't want to depend on a woman whose career was so important.

She took a bite, the fork entering her pretty mouth, and when he pulled it away he noticed that she'd closed her eyes. She savored that bite of cake the way he wanted to savor her. He wanted to linger over every curve of her body, wanted to explore each inch until he knew her better than she knew herself. And he would.

If she trusted him, he'd do his best to live up to that for as long as he could. He knew himself well enough to know that eventually he'd let her down.

He'd done that most of his life when it came to relationships, but for the first time he didn't want that to happen. He wanted to be a man that she'd always be able to look up to.

"Thank you," she said. "That was delicious."

"You're welcome," he said. He put the fork down and signaled for the check.

He hadn't realized that by playing games with her, by seducing her slowly and trying to find her weaknesses, he'd find his own.

With her wide violet eyes and her full red lips, she'd drawn him into her web. And a part of him would be happy to stay there. But a bigger part of him knew that weakness lay with emotional dependency.

Not the small weaknesses that made up character flaws but the bigger ones, like needing Ainsley, that were something that could cost him the competition with Henry and Geoff. And possibly the success of the retail group.

Ainsley was dangerous.

Looking at her sitting across the table from him, it was hard to believe it, but she was. She made him want things that weren't work-related. She made him want to sit at home at night in front of a fire with her curled up by his side.

She made him want to think about the future with her and maybe having some kids. And that was a very frightening picture. Being a parent and being successful just didn't go together.

Nine

Finding herself sitting outside her house with Steven again, she had an odd sense of déjà vu. Her emotions were all in a jumble and she was worried about what she might do or say. For the first time in a long time she felt out of control. She wanted Steven and that desire was taking over every part of her.

She wanted to be smart and charming—Rosalind Russell in *His Girl Friday*. But she was afraid that if she opened her mouth, she'd come off as more unsure and awkward.

"Haven't we been here before?" she asked.

"I believe we have," he said.

He'd turned the car off and turned to face her. It was a lane dimly lit by streetlamps. The light from one of them illuminated his face but kept part of it in shadow.

He was a mystery to her. Even after all her research about him, she still couldn't figure him out. He sat with his body turned toward her and his arm resting on the steering wheel.

"Invite me in," he said at last.

She was going to, but why did he make everything he said sound like an order? "Why are you so bossy?"

"Because men who aren't don't get what they want."

"What do you want?" she asked.

"You really don't know?"

She did know what he wanted, but somehow saying it out loud would make it too real and she wasn't sure she wanted to do that. "To come inside."

"Indeed."

"Would you like a drink?"

"Would you?"

She laughed. "I think I need one. You tie me up in knots."

"Do I? I think that's a good thing," he said.

"Why?"

"You do the same thing to me," he said, reaching over to caress her face.

"Oh."

"Oh?" He leaned in. "You have the most kissable mouth."

He rubbed his lips against hers gently. The kiss was nothing like the one he'd given her earlier—so demanding and bold. This was soft and seduced her by degrees. Slowly. He kissed her as if he had all the time in the world, which he probably did. They had all night.

He pulled back, opened his door and came around to open hers. She gave him her hand and then climbed out of the low-slung sports car. She led the way up her walk to her front door. This time she didn't drop the keys. She wasn't nervous at all.

A strange calm had settled over her when he'd kissed her so softly. Steven was more than her obsession; he was a man she had come to know a little better over the last week.

She unlocked her door and stepped over the threshold. The lights were on in the living room and cast a warm, inviting glow into the foyer. Steven stepped inside, closing the door behind him. She led the way, almost kicking off her shoes in the hallway, but she remembered at the last moment that she had company and according to her mother, men didn't like messy women.

"What can I get you?"

"You," he said.

As he pulled her into his arms, she wrapped her arms around his waist and rested her head on his chest. She suspected that he wanted the embrace to be something more than this, but right now this was all she could do. She took comfort from the feel of his chest under her cheek. From the feel of her arms around his waist. From the scent of his natural musk with each inhalation.

She was tired of denying herself everything she wanted. It was one thing to resist dessert but something altogether different to deny herself the chance to be with Steven. She had fantasized about him every night since their first date.

His hands stroked her back gently. The touch was comforting at first and then the timbre changed and it became seductive. His hands swept lower each time, his fingers caressing her back with each stroke.

She tipped her head to the left and he kissed her first on the forehead and then let his lips move down the side of her face. Small, nibbling kisses that felt light, almost as if she were imagining them.

Then he reached her ear. His tongue traced the shell of her ear and she shivered as darts of awareness shot down her neck and arms. Her nipples tightened and her breasts felt fuller.

"Remember when I kissed you by my car," he said, his hot breath going directly into her ear. She shuddered with the memories of that kiss and how inflamed she'd felt.

"Yes," she said.

"I'm going to kiss you like that again, but this time I'm not stopping until I'm buried hilt-deep inside of you."

Her inner body clenched and she felt a humid warmth bloom between her legs. She shifted around until she could look him in the eyes. "Good. I want that, Steven. I want everything you have to give me."

Ainsley realized that he couldn't make promises. She might not believe him if he did. She trusted him because he didn't make promises he wouldn't keep. And she wouldn't ask him to.

For this night, she wanted only to be in his arms. She didn't need to think about the future. She'd never been one to think about forever. Losing weight and changing how she looked on the outside hadn't changed her on the inside.

"Do you want that drink?" she asked, not sure how to proceed.

"No," he said. "I don't want anything but you. But if a drink will relax you, I'll have one, too."

She hesitated. She wished she could just take him by the hand and lead him to her bedroom, but she definitely needed a drink. She pulled away. "Wine okay?"

"Yes," he said.

She left him in the living room and went into her kitchen to get the bottle she'd chilled earlier. She savored white wine. Hopefully, he liked the dry taste of pinot grigio.

He was moving around in the living room and then she heard the mellow sound of Otis Redding. She had a huge collection of old-time R&B. It was her favorite, and she was surprised that he'd chosen it. But the music relaxed her a bit more.

She poured them each a glass of wine and then took a deep breath before going back out into the living room. It would be so much easier for her if Steven Devonshire were just another man. Instead he was *the* man. Oh, my God, she thought. He was the one she wanted out of all the other men. And that made this night so important to her. A first kiss only happened once—and that had been eminently memorable. So did a first-time sharing each other's bodies. She wanted that to be perfect as well.

Steven knew he could easily push Ainsley's shyness aside by kissing her until she had no choice but to be swept down the hall and into her own bed. But he wanted her to want to be there, comfortable in her own skin.

He loosened his tie and undid the first button of his dress shirt, then walked around her living room to the Bose stereo system where music played softly. In a cabinet next to the unit were her CDs and they were all lined up in alphabetical order. She had an eclectic collection, including a lot of old rhythm and blues CDs. Otis Redding, Ray Charles, Marvin Gaye and some of the classic Italian-American singers like Louis Prima, Frank Sinatra and Dean Martin.

There was Cold Play and Green Day in there, too. And some newer artists he'd never heard of. Seeing her music collection showed him that he'd only scratched the surface of who she was. Ainsley wasn't a woman who was easy to know. He put on an Otis Redding album, turned off the larger overhead light and turned on the lamp on the side table.

The ambient light created the intimate mood he wanted. He thought about everything he knew about Ainsley, how she'd been fat, and that had virtually defined her. He'd been thinking a lot about the woman who'd interviewed him five years ago. He'd been telling her the truth when he'd said that she'd seemed invisible. But he had started to wonder if he'd done anything to contribute to that. Had he simply ignored her because she wasn't slim?

He couldn't change the past, but he intended to make sure that she knew he wanted her now. She'd have no doubts that he loved her and her body. He'd do everything in his power to make sure that she got lost in his embrace. That she didn't have time to think about her past or any of her imagined flaws.

She came back into the room and hesitated in the doorway. She held two glasses of wine and her expression was a mix of bravado and desire. Clearly, she wanted him— probably with the same intensity as he wanted her, though he found that hard to believe. No way could she want him as much as he wanted her.

He walked over to her and took one wineglass from her.

"I hope you like white wine."

"I do," he said. He put his hand on the small of her back and led her into the living room. She perched delicately on the edge of the love seat, her legs crossed demurely, and he felt as if he were back in his aunt Lucy's drawing room.

He took her hand and drew her to her feet. He might not be much of a dancer, but he could sway with the best of them. And he knew the surest way to coax Ainsley out of her reserve was by putting his arms around her.

"To a lovely evening," he said, raising his glass to hers.

She clinked her glass to his and took a sip. So did he, draining half the glass and setting it on the side table. He took hers and did the same. Then he came back behind her and pulled her into his arms. Her back against his chest.

He lowered his head next to hers and whispered sweet nothings to her, bending his knees to spoon her while they were standing there together. He wrapped his arms around her, letting his thumb and hand rest under her right breast, his other hand on her abdomen.

He swayed back and forth to the music and felt her relax against him. He put his mouth on her neck right at the base and kissed her, then let her feel the edge of his teeth.

He felt her breast jump in his hand and she shifted her hips to rub against his erection. He hardened and his blood ran heavier. Every instinct he had told him to hurry this up.

But he'd learned over time that he enjoyed his orgasm more if he drew it out. He continued swaying with her and found the buttons of her blouse with his left hand. Slowly he undid them. He left the blouse tucked into her skirt but unfastened it all the way.

Her skin was lily white and soft. So soft that he couldn't stop caressing her. He traced a path up the center of her body from where her belly button was to her rib cage to the sin-red bra that encased her full breasts. He traced his finger over the underwire that supported her. Then he skimmed the edge of the lace where it met the creamy skin of her chest. He let his forefinger dip under the fabric to caress her creamy breasts.

She rotated her shoulders, seeming to want his touch to move to her breasts, but he wasn't ready for that yet.

He nibbled on her ear and kept his finger moving slowly over that part of her breast. Then he inched his way to the velvety skin of her nipple, touching her carefully when she jerked in his arms. Her hips swiveled against his and her hands came to his wrist to grip him.

"I want to see you," she said, trying to turn in his embrace.

"Not yet."

"When?"

"When you are totally a slave to love," he said.

She tipped her head back so that their eyes met. The action thrust her breasts out and made his finger run over her nipple. She shuddered again.

"I already am," she said.

"Not like you will be," he said.

He pinched her nipple lightly, watching carefully to see if it was too much for her. But she liked it. She bit her lower lip and her hips moved against his again.

He slid his hand around to the zipper in the side of her skirt and drew it down. The skirt slid slowly over her hips and then fell to her ankles. He glanced down to see that she had on a minute pair of panties that matched her bra. But above that she had on a garter belt that held up her hose. He took a step back and pushed her blouse off her shoulders.

He walked around in front of her. She was an image straight from a wet dream. She was hot and sexy, and as she stood there in her high heels and her decadent underwear, suddenly a slow seduction seemed like a very stupid idea. All he wanted was to rip those little panties from her body and make her his. She belonged to him.

Possessiveness wasn't his style, but he wanted every inch of Ainsley, and he was going to claim it all.

* * *

Ainsley's body was on fire. Steven called to her. When he finally entered her line of vision, she was surprised that he was still dressed. She didn't feel vulnerable, as she had expected to standing in front of him, because of the lust in his eyes. He wanted her and he couldn't stop looking at her.

The bulge of his erection also made her feel feminine, sexy. Like a woman who held power over her man. And for tonight Steven was *her* man. She started to take his clothes off, but he held up his finger. "Not yet."

"Why?" she asked.

"I'm not done looking at you yet."

She felt a sliver of fear but it passed quickly and she put her hands on her waist and cocked out one hip. "Take your time."

"I will," he said. "I can't believe you're mine."

"Am I yours?" she asked. No man had claimed her before. She'd had one lover before Steven—that had been in her early twenties, and now she was thirty. The sex had been okay but she knew that Steven was the type of man who'd make her come. Sex wasn't going to just be okay. She knew she'd never look at him the same way after this.

"Yes."

He put his hands on her shoulders and held her where she was. He lowered his head and kissed her. It was the same kiss he'd given her by the car that first night but at the same time a million times more intense. He didn't let their bodies touch at all. Just used his lips and teeth and tongue to make her his and she was helpless to do anything but respond.

She reached between their bodies and took his tie off. Drawing it out of his collar and dropping it on the floor by her skirt. Then she started unbuttoning his shirt, her fingernails scraping against the wall of his chest.

He shuddered and pulled back from her. "Do that again."

She did, scraping her nails down his body all the way to his waistband. The skin on his stomach jumped as her touch went lower. She pushed his shirt from his shoulders and then realized she'd left his cuff links on. The shirt bound his hands. And he couldn't touch her.

"Now you are *my* slave," she said. "And you are one fine-looking slave."

She walked around him and stood behind him as he had positioned himself behind her. She touched him from his shoulders down the center of his back and then cupped his tight buttocks. She put one arm around his chest and drew him back against her. The other arm she put around his lean waist and then she went up on her tiptoes and bit him lightly on his neck.

She unzipped his pants and let her hand drift lower inside his underwear to caress him. She rubbed her fingers up and down his length and then massaged the crown of his erection. She felt him shiver in her arms and she smiled to herself.

She was just following what he'd done to her. She unfastened his belt, drawing it slowly from around his lean waist.

She reached into the opening of his pants, touched him through his underwear and then found the opening in his boxers and let her fingers sweep inside and stroke up and down his length. He turned in her arms and knocked her off balance, but he caught her quickly, lifting her up in his arms and going to the love seat. He set her on her feet and pushed his pants and underwear down his legs. Then he took off his cuff links and shrugged out of his shirt.

He stood before her, an Adonis of a man—perfectly formed. His erection stood out from his body and she felt a rush of pure desire as she realized that she had turned him on.

"Take your panties off," he said, his voice low and raspy.

She hesitated for a second and then kicked off her shoes. She started to undo the garter belt, but he stopped her.

"Leave that on."

"Okay." She got her panties as far as her knees when he stopped her again.

"Turn around."

"Why?"

"Because I love your behind," he said. And I want to see you when you bend over.

A shudder of awareness ripped through her at his words and she did as he asked. As soon as she bent forward she felt his hands slide over her back. Then his nails did the same down the line of her spine.

She stepped out of her panties and when she stood up, he kept the pressure on her back. "Stay like this."

She wasn't sure what he had in mind, but she did as he said.

"Are you on the Pill?"

"No. Sorry, I didn't think about protection," she said, trying to turn around and stand up.

"Don't worry, love, I did," he said. He reached for his pants and pulled a condom out of the pocket. She heard the packet rip. Then she felt the tip of his erection against her. He held her hips in his hands and leaned forward so that his chest settled against her back. He reached around her. Held her wrapped in his arms as he eased himself into her body.

Just the tip in and out until she thought she was going to die from wanting him.

He reached lower between her legs and parted her nether lips. His finger rubbed her up and down until she felt like she was going to come. She couldn't stop moving her hips. Couldn't stop trying to get more of his hardness inside of her.

"Steven, take me."

"Yes, ma'am," he said. He bit down on her neck and thrust himself deep inside her. Ripples of her climax washed over her and she was a shivery mass of nerves.

He continued to thrust into her, driving her to another orgasm, and the third time she came, he did as well.

He fell back on the couch and held her in his arms as they both came back to themselves. She curled herself into his arms, feeling more vulnerable than she ever believed she could. For the first time the girl who never thought she'd find a man to love realized that she wanted this one.

Ten

Ainsley woke up at 2:00 a.m. and knew she wasn't alone. She bolted upright in bed, jerking all the covers with her.

"Love?"

"Steven?"

"Who else would it be?"

"I don't know," she said feeling very silly. But she had never shared her bed with anyone.

Steven stroked his hand along her spine and then drew her down into his arms. He was warm and her head seemed to find the perfect spot on his shoulder. He put his arm around her shoulder and she lay quietly trying to go back to sleep. It was hard.

Way too hard to figure out how to sleep with this man…

"What are you thinking about?" he asked.

"That I've never slept with anyone," she said. An only

child, she'd never been scared of the dark and as a child her parents' bedroom had been off-limits to her.

"Never? Not even as a child?" he asked.

"Nope. My parents believed in kids in their own beds. And I wasn't very social as a child, so I didn't do sleepovers." She had been chubby even as a child, but more than that she'd simply liked being by herself. She didn't mix well with others. She'd been more interested in the world she'd created in her head. A world where she could be a princess and everyone liked her.

She hadn't thought of that in years. Thought of that painful time in her childhood.

"So I'm your first?" Steven said.

He was in so many ways. The first man she'd made love to, not the boy-man she'd had sex with before. She tipped her head up, but her room was dark. She wished she could see his expression better.

"Is that good?"

He shrugged, dislodging her from his shoulder. He didn't say anything else. What did this mean to him? What did it mean to her? She knew better than to make decisions in the middle of the night, but a part of her wanted to. She wanted to figure Steven out so she wouldn't get hurt, but a part of her was afraid that it was too late for that.

She was already falling for him.

She wasn't going to ask, but she wanted to know. Did she mean more to Steven than this one night or even a series of nights that added up to weeks before he moved on?

She had no idea what any of his behavior meant.

"Are you sleeping?" she whispered.

"With your hand stroking my belly button? No, I'm not sleeping."

She hadn't realized she was doing that, but sure enough her hand was low on his stomach. She stopped moving it.

"Don't stop. I like it."

She started moving her hand again, and noticed that his hand was caressing her arm. There was nothing overtly sexual in the touching; it was two people comforting each other, she thought.

"I haven't slept with that many people, either. I tend to go back to my place instead of sleeping over."

"Really? Why?"

"I don't like mornings. It's always awkward."

That revealed a lot to her. He didn't like to stay because though sex was okay, anything resembling a relationship made him uncomfortable. "Awkward how?"

"Normally I have work to do and have to leave early and—you don't want to hear this."

Yet she did want to. She didn't want to know the details of his past affairs, but she did want to know why he left. Or was she simply drawing a conclusion based on her perceptions of who he was? Work was one reason but she suspected that was an excuse. Steven was the CEO of a large company. If he came in late, no one was going to say a word to him.

"Work's not the reason you leave," she said. "You leave because you don't want to stay."

His hand stopped moving on her arm and she wondered if she'd said too much. Even so, she didn't care if she had. This affair with Steven was something totally new to her. She wasn't going to hedge her bets or try to play it safe. If he didn't want her once they'd slept together, she wanted to know now.

"I think you're right. I've never given it much thought.

Just got up and left when I wanted to. Work calls… My job is my life…"

"And no woman could compete with that," she finished for him.

"That's right."

She lay still next to him, knowing that she was going to ask the next question whether it was wise or not.

"What about me?"

He turned on the bed so they lay facing each other. He put both arms around her—one around her neck the other over her waist and drew her flush against his body.

"I have no clue. You aren't like anyone else."

That didn't reassure her at all and in fact raised more doubts about being with Steven. He wasn't an easy man to get close to. With each step she took toward him, he found a new way to freeze her out and keep her at arm's length.

She wanted to ask more questions, but she had a feeling that was all he'd admit to her. She closed her eyes and enjoyed being so close to him. She put her arm over his waist and tucked her head under his chin.

He held her like that until they both drifted off to sleep. Ainsley tried not to let it mean too much that he held her as tightly as she held him.

Steven woke to bright sunlight streaming in through some filmy curtains. Ainsley was curled by his side. He eased out of bed to go to the bathroom and saw his clothes where he'd left them on the overstuffed chair that sat in the corner of her bedroom.

He almost walked over and got dressed. He could leave. Nothing was keeping him here. But as he looked at Ainsley sleeping in her bed, her hand reaching out to where he'd lain, he couldn't do it.

He didn't want her to wake up alone. He had the feeling from what she'd said last night that she'd led a very solitary life.

Dammit, he cared about her. Yet he didn't want emotional entanglements. How had this happened? She was a woman who looked like she shouldn't have touched any of his emotions. But she had.

And that was the problem.

"Steven?" she called his name as she sat up in bed. She wore a pretty flower-printed nightgown and her hair was tousled around her shoulders. Her eyes were sleepy as she tried to see him. Last night he'd learned that she wore contacts—something as new to her as her weight loss.

He saw her reaching for her nightstand and the glasses she had set on the top last night.

"I'm here."

"Are you leaving?" she asked.

"Do you want me to?" he asked. It would be so much easier if she said yes. He could walk away and he'd never forget the time he'd spent with her, but this encounter would fade into a memory. Nothing more.

"I would like it if you came back to bed."

He smiled. He went back to the bed and sat down next to her.

"Happy now?"

"Yes," she said, squinting up at him.

"Put your glasses on," he said.

"No. They aren't attractive at all. I'll go put my contacts in."

That made no sense to him. "You don't have to."

He reached for her glasses and handed them to her. She held them for a minute and then put them on. "There you are," she said lightly.

"Here I am."

He leaned in and kissed her softly. "Good morning."

"Good morning," she said.

"Why didn't you want to put your glasses on?"

"I…they are part of the old me. Not this new person that you found attractive."

He crossed his arms over his chest. He was getting a picture of Ainsley as a woman who hid her true self from the world. "So who's the real Ainsley? The sexy temptress I met last night or this shy woman I'm seeing this morning."

She bit her lower lip. "I don't know. I would have said this is me, but last night I felt comfortable in my body for the first time. I'm not talking about just since I lost weight—I mean ever. I've never felt like my skin fit me. Last night, when I was in your arms, I found myself."

She shook her head. "Oh, God, I sound like a moron."

He laughed, but deep inside he knew that being with him wasn't an easy decision for Ainsley.

Hurting her was the very last thing he wanted. He had to be careful if he didn't intend to lose his heart or let his emotions overwhelm him. And the only way to protect himself was to make sure she didn't get too involved with him.

He wanted to go back to bed with her but he wasn't sure that was wise. He'd only brought two condoms with him last night. It would take a box to continue this affair with Ainsley. Twice wasn't nearly enough to get his fill of her.

Ainsley was finding her confidence as a woman in his arms. What she'd said about finding herself made sense to him. Because he'd noted that change in her. She dressed like a confident woman who knew the power of her sexuality but until last night he didn't think she really had.

"I have a meeting with Henry and Geoff in an hour," he said.

"I am actually going to be late if I don't leave in ten minutes. Freddie is never going to let me live this down."

"What does he have to say about this? I thought he worked for you."

"He does, but he's also one of my best friends."

"You're friends with a man?"

She laughed at him and punched him lightly in the shoulder. "Yes, I am. Don't you have any women friends?"

He didn't. If pressed, he might describe Dinah as a friend, but she was really more of an employee. "No, I don't. And you don't need any guy friends while you're with me. I can provide all the testosterone you need."

"Steven, I'm an independent woman and I'm not about to let you tell me who I can be friends with. I'm not going to be sleeping around, but Freddie and I are still going to stay friends."

"Fine."

This was precisely why he avoided relationships. Because he was always afraid of losing the very thing he wanted. And he hated to admit that he might need anything from Ainsley other than sex, but she was different. And he disliked this feeling of needing to be the only man in her life. It was crazy.

She looked up at him with her wide violet eyes and he was very afraid that she'd complicate his life. That his life had changed so much last night when he'd taken her in his arms.

He didn't want his life turned upside down, so he left a few minutes later when she got into the shower. He wasn't a man who was jealous or possessive, yet Ainsley awakened both emotions in him. Why?

As he drove through the early morning traffic, he had doubts. Why was Ainsley affecting him this way? He had always been able to put women in their place in his life and just keep on his path to total world domination. But she was playing with his head and he was very afraid for his heart.

He knew that he couldn't insist on crazy things, like forbidding a woman to have male friends, and he had never done that with his other girlfriends. So why with her? What made her so different?

To a man used to always having the answers, this situation was thoroughly unsettling. Until he knew why Ainsley was affecting him this deeply, he needed to keep his distance. He didn't want to end up with a messy personal life the way Malcolm Devonshire had.

Ainsley couldn't talk to Freddie about last night no matter how many times he asked. Steven had left while she was in the shower. And even though she knew he had a meeting this morning, she'd expected him to say goodbye. She knew he had things to do and she hadn't expected him to just hang out at her house all day, but leaving without a word…well, she knew he was running away.

It shouldn't matter, but it did. She'd taken a big risk last night by having sex with him and the reward had been better than she had expected. She'd never had an orgasm like that before or that many. She'd also never felt as appealing to the opposite sex as she had when she'd been in his arms.

But she'd never been as disappointed in a man as she

had been when she'd come out of the shower and realized that Steven had left.

It had been a cowardly thing to do. Frankly, she'd expected better of him. When her staff meeting ended, she stood up and left the room. Freddie followed close on her heels.

"Hold up, boss lady. We need to talk."

She shook her head.

"Nope, I'm not going to let you get away with that. We've been friends too long for you to hide things from me."

Ainsley stared at her friend. He wore his short hair spiked up this morning. He had on a pair of gabardine slacks, combat boots and a vintage Stones T-shirt. His round, horn-rimmed glasses were for show, but the expression in his eyes was sincere.

"I can't talk about it. Not yet. We can do drinks later in the week and we can talk then."

"Are you sure?"

She nodded. "I'm too raw about this. I have a magazine to run. I can't afford to let this bother me."

"What happened?"

"Nothing," she said, aware that she was making this into something bigger than it was. But she'd let Steven see the most vulnerable side of her and he'd left without saying anything.

"Fine. Drinks Friday. I'm not going to let you get away with keeping this in."

"Sounds good. Now get to work."

He hugged her and then walked away. The fact that he'd hugged her told her that she needed to get to her office before anyone else noticed that the ultra-efficient boss they'd come to know wasn't herself.

Cathy had left a stack of messages for her and there were

proof sheets that she needed to sign off on, but all she could do was think about last night. She spun her chair around to face the window, but found no solace in the spectacular view.

St. Peter's now reminded her of Steven.

She turned back to her desk, opened her e-mail account and thought for a long minute before she started writing to Steven.

Was there an emergency this morning? Leaving without saying goodbye was cowardly. I thought you were a different kind of man.

She hit Send before she gave in to her anger further and called him an ass. Twenty minutes later her cell phone rang.

She glanced at the caller ID to see Steven's name. She didn't want to talk to him, but she realized that calling him a coward and avoiding his call would make her one.

"This is Ainsley," she said as she answered her phone.

"I'm sorry about this morning. I just felt the walls closing in and I had to get out of there. It wasn't you," he said. "It was me."

"What does that mean? Walls closing in?"

Silence buzzed on the open line for a long minute. "I wanted to stay. I wanted to come into the shower with you and make love to you—to hell with the consequences. And that's not who I am."

She flushed at his words. Realized that he wanted her with the same intensity as she wanted him.

His fears mirrored her own. They were both so used to going their own way that coming together seemed like it would be an immense challenge. A challenge that might be too much for them.

"I feel the same way, Steven. But at the end of the day, you're worth the risk to me. That's why I called you on your actions. If I'm not worth the risk to you then fine—just say so and we can end this now."

"And if I think you are?" he asked.

"Then we try to figure this out. We figure out how to make this relationship work for us."

"Relationship?"

"Yes. I don't want to be one in a line of lovers you have. I have too much respect for myself to get involved with a man like you unless there is more than just sex."

"A man like me?" he asked.

She had said too much. Steven was the kind of man she could fall in love with and saying that to him would leave her feeling like she'd stripped her clothes off in the center of the office.

She thought for a moment. No risk, no reward, she thought. "I could fall for you."

"Ainsley…"

"Don't say anything else. I know you aren't the kind of man to fall in love, but I am that kind of woman. If you aren't looking for at least some kind of solid relationship, then I have to end this now."

"I don't want to see you hurt, but I have to tell you I'm not…I've never been a forever kind of guy. But I'm not ready to let you go, either."

"Is it me or any woman?"

"Damn. I can't believe we are having this conversation on the phone," he said.

"Stop stalling, Steven. Is it me?"

"Hell, no, Ainsley. It's not you. I'm not ready to let you go. So yes, I want to pursue this."

The not-loving thing she'd deal with later. It was enough for her that he wanted to keep seeing her. Because she wasn't ready to let him go, either. "Okay. That's all I wanted to know."

"Glad you're happy," he said.

"I want you to be, too," she said.

"I will be when we're together again. I have to go to Berne so I'll be out of town for a few days."

"To see your mum?"

"Yes. She's busy at the accelerator and won't answer her cell," Steven said.

"Is it an emergency?" she asked. "Something with your family?"

"No. It's you. I told you I'd get my half brothers and our mothers to talk to you and mum won't unless I go there and ask her in person."

He was doing it for her. Suddenly it didn't matter that he'd left her this morning. No matter how confident Steven seemed, this "relationship" between them was throwing him off his normal game. She wasn't sure that was a good thing. The two of them might be destined for something greater—maybe to fall in love or perhaps to destroy each other.

Eleven

Steven entered the secure facility in Berne and found Roman waiting for him. The older man hugged him and greeted him like an old friend.

"Hello, Steven. Lynn will be up here in a few minutes. How was the drive?"

"Long," he said. He could have flown, but he needed time in the car alone to try to figure out why he was doing this. He'd always been careful to give his mum space, never wanted to be too clingy to her and yet he was in Berne because Ainsley needed an answer. He'd hurt her by walking out on her.

He'd made up the excuse that his Moretti roadster was made to be driven. So he'd taken it on this cross-continent trip. But on the drive he'd had a chance to put things into perspective and had made sense of his decision to do the articles. They were for the good of his company, not just for Ainsley. Now he felt more like his old self.

Ainsley had overwhelmed him during the night they spent together, but he had decided that it was only because it had been the first time they made love that he'd reacted like that. Once he got back to London and saw her again, she'd be like all the other women he'd dated. She was hot, but she wasn't any different from any other woman he'd slept with.

"Steven," his mum said from the doorway.

"Hi, Mum," he said, walking over to her. She hugged him close and held him for a few minutes before letting go. She always did that. He didn't know why she held him for so long, but a part of him liked it. When she hugged him he felt like she was just his mum, not a brilliant physicist everyone in the world wanted a piece of.

"I'm sorry I couldn't call you," she said.

"It's okay. I needed to get in my car and drive," he said.

She laughed. His mum had changed very little over the years. She was tallish, almost five-foot-eight, and had thick, curly brown hair with streaks of deep red woven through it that she wore in a very casual bun at the back of her head. Tendrils of hair escaped it to drift around her face. She had on her lab coat and the earrings he'd given her for her last birthday.

Roman watched them both, as he always did, like an indulgent father figure. Steven suspected that Roman was Lynn's lover, but his mother had never said anything about a romantic relationship between them so he kept that thought to himself.

"Do you have time for me?" he asked his mum.

"I've got an hour, sweetheart. I'm all yours."

"Want to go for a drive?" he asked her.

"I'd love to. I haven't left this facility in days," she said. She glanced over at Roman. "Will you call me if anything happens?"

"Of course. Enjoy your time with Steven. I'll take care of everything here."

She nodded and waved three fingers at Roman before linking her arm through Steven's. "Let's go."

He led the way to his car and got her seated. Then he put down the top of the convertible.

"Why are you in Berne?" she asked as he drove the car to a park that his mother suggested.

He parked the car and they got out and walked around the grounds. His mother was always very touchy-feely when they were together and he remembered as a small boy how much he'd enjoyed the fact that when she left the lab, she'd given him her full attention.

He suspected a part of her knew that he was lonely from spending so much time by himself. He hated how weak he felt when he was with his mum. He'd always wanted to make their time together last longer but yet, eventually he'd just found a way to let her go. It had meant shutting down everything, especially the hope that she'd stop being a physicist.

"Remember when Malcolm contacted you about me?" he asked, knowing that she would need all the details before she could make a decision about doing the interview with Ainsley's magazine.

"Yes. Did that work out?"

"Well, he laid out a challenge for all three of his heirs. We're all competing to see who can make the most profit in one of the business units and I need your help," he said.

"I don't know anything about business," she said.

"Mum, is it my first day being your son?"

She laughed. "I guess not. What can I do?"

"I've arranged for *Fashion Quarterly* to do a series of articles about the Everest Group. And the editor-in-chief wants her writer to interview each of our mums. As a fashion magazine, they want to talk to the women involved."

"About Malcolm?" Lynn asked.

"I don't really know. Maybe about your work."

"Is this important to you?" she asked.

Steven thought about it. No one had been important to him, but he knew that Ainsley was. He didn't want to be the reason why her article didn't fly.

"Yes, she is."

"*She* is?"

"I meant *it*. The articles are important. They will reintroduce the world to a brand that they may think of as passé."

"Don't even try it, Steven. You said *she*. Do you like the writer who is doing the articles?"

"No, Mum. I like the editor-in-chief."

"What's she like?" Lynn asked.

"She's American."

"Oh. What's that mean?"

He wanted to laugh. "She's different. She works in publishing and she's smart and funny."

"Sounds perfect for you. Did you take her to meet Aunt Lucy?"

"No. I'm not going to, either. You know how Aunt Lucy can be."

"I know she loves us," Lynn said.

"Yes, she does. But she can be pushy. She calls me once a week."

"Me, too," his mum said with a laugh. "Poor Lucy, stuck with two workaholics as family."

"Yeah, poor Lucy," he said.

"Do you ever resent me for the way your childhood was?" she asked.

"No," he said. "Why?"

"Roman said that I compartmentalize people. And I thought about when you were little and you wanted to spend time with me but I was always in the lab."

"You were the best mum you could be."

She shrugged. "That's true, but was it enough?"

"I have no idea. You're the only mum I have."

She smiled at him. "I don't want you to feel like I ignored you because I didn't want you."

This wasn't about him at all, but something was bothering his mother. He wondered if being with Roman had made her realize that family was more important to her than she'd acknowledged. "I always knew that your job takes all your attention. And you're brilliant at what you do, so that's okay."

She leaned over and kissed his cheek. "Thank you, Steven."

"You're welcome."

Her watch alarm went off. "I have to get back."

They walked back to the car and when they got there, Steven asked her, "Will you do the interview?"

"Only if the writer e-mails me the questions."

"That's all I ask. Bye, Mum," he said, wanting to be the one who said goodbye first.

"Steven?"

"Yes?"

"I…I've been thinking that maybe I didn't do a very

good job of showing you that life is about more than work."

He didn't respond to that. "Why does that matter?"

"If you like this woman, don't make the mistakes that your father and I did. You might find yourself looking back on life with regrets."

"What do you regret?"

"Not making more time for you," she said.

"Why now?" he asked her.

"Roman asked me to marry him. And I…I've said yes."

"Good. Congratulations," he said. But inside a door was closing. His mum and Roman would have their world together. Their life would be in the lab most of the time and that was something Steven couldn't be a part of.

"Thanks, sweetheart. I want you to be happy, too, Steven. Don't wait until it's almost too late to realize that life is more than work."

He nodded. He doubted that he could change the way he was. And he wasn't too sure he'd ever be able to be with a woman like Ainsley. He already knew that she made him react with jealousy and that wasn't the thing he needed to keep a calm head and stay focused on business.

Yet at the same time he'd always been determined not to repeat the mistakes his parents had made. He was going to pursue Ainsley and see if she could be the missing link in his relationship DNA.

At this moment everything seemed easy, but he knew it wouldn't be. He didn't love her. In fact he wasn't sure he had the capacity to love. He only knew that he wanted her and it was damn hard to work when he kept thinking about her. And he thought—knew—that Ainsley felt the same way about him.

Having her officially as his own would take away the doubt and hopefully the jealousy. He called Ainsley's office and found out that she was in Milan. Good, he thought. That gave him the time he needed to plan.

His mother's engagement to Roman had planted the seeds of his own engagement. To Ainsley. As his mum had said when he'd left…don't wait until it's too late.

Ainsley flew back from a meeting in Milan and arrived at Heathrow close to midnight. She was tired and wanted nothing more than to go home and sleep in Steven's arms. But she hadn't seen him in over three weeks. The logistics of a relationship like theirs was harder to figure out than she'd expected.

Steven had gotten his mother to agree to the interview, and she was using every contact she had to try to get in to see Malcolm Devonshire. But she had almost given up. Okay, that was a lie; she wasn't going to give up on getting him until the issue was on the newsstands.

She walked down the gateway wheeling her laptop bag behind her. It was one of those with a compartment for carry-on clothing as well and she found it was perfect for the short-haul business trips she took a lot of the time. Especially in the spring when all of the fashion weeks were in full swing and she traveled every week.

She turned on her BlackBerry as soon as she was down the gateway and found a message waiting for her from Cathy, informing her that a car would be picking her up at the curb.

It was times like this when she really adored her assistant. She was too tired to even think of dealing with a cab. She walked out of the terminal building, past the barriers and saw Steven standing by his car, leaning on the hood and watching for her.

She was so happy to see him. She had forgotten how much she liked his handsome face and that half smile of his made her feel like she really was home.

"Are you my ride?" she asked.

"I am. I figured the only way we'd be able to see each other was in the middle of the night when the rest of the world doesn't need us.

"Is that the only bag you have?" he asked.

"Yes. I hate to wait for luggage, so I ship it wherever I'm going."

Steven walked beside her and a part of her liked it. He opened the door for her and she climbed inside, relaxing back against the leather bucket seats as he climbed into the car.

He was playing music by one of the newer Everest Group recording artists, Steph Cordo. "This song is so popular right now. You must be excited to have a company artist doing so well."

"No, I'm not. I'm trying to beat Henry financially," Steven said.

"You are? Is that one of the stipulations of the deal with Malcolm? I know you are all competing."

"Yes. How was Milan?"

"Busy. But it was a productive visit. We're getting ready for the fashion shows coming up in the fall."

"Do you go to them all?"

"Usually. We sponsor a runway for upcoming artists and do other events," she said.

"Do you like it?"

"Most of the time. When I get home I generally take a week off to recover."

She glanced out the window and realized that they weren't heading toward Notting Hill. They were on the A3 heading south. "Where are we going?"

"My place."

"Oh."

"Is that okay?"

"Yes," she said. "I'm going to need a ride to work tomorrow."

"No, you won't. You're taking the day off."

"I am?"

"Yes. As luck would have it I have the day off, as well. I thought we'd spend it together."

She smiled to herself. "That sounds wonderful."

Her eyes drifted closed for a minute and when he stopped the car, rousing her, she found they were in a large rustic garage.

"We are at my country house in Cobham," Steven said.

She had spent little time outside London and she wished it were daylight so she could see the Surrey countryside surrounding his house. "I slept the entire way. Sorry about that."

"You were tired," he said. He got out of the car and took her bag from the trunk. He led the way up the path from the garage to the house. It was very modern and large, especially compared to the townhomes she was used to.

They entered through a side door into the kitchen. It was outfitted with all the modern conveniences and a large restaurant-grade stove. "Do you cook?"

"It's a hobby. My aunt Lucy is a chef and she taught me when I was little."

"Did you spend a lot of time with her?" Ainsley asked. All the articles she'd read about him in magazines and on the Internet had been about his business interests and nothing had been about family.

"Yes, whenever my mum was needed in Berne. She's been working on the particle accelerator for years."

"Is she working on the God particle?"

"Mum started working on it with Peter Higgs. He found the Higgs Boson. Then she started doing her own research. It's been her life's work. I'm sure she'll talk to your writer about it, but only via e-mail."

"That will be great," she said.

He led the way through the house. She had a vague impression of dark blue hues and a very British-looking den before he led her upstairs.

"Spend a lot of time here?"

The master suite had a large king-size bed in the middle of it and an en suite bathroom. There was a flat-screen, LCD TV on the wall and a love seat in front of it with a large padded ottoman.

"It's my retreat," he admitted.

"Do you bring a lot of people here?" she asked.

"You're the first," he said.

Ainsley didn't want to read too much into that. After all, this was only the third time they'd been together, but she couldn't help but feel special.

Steven had been busy over the last three weeks but mostly he'd been aware of how much he'd missed Ainsley. She was a busy woman and though she'd made a big deal about having a relationship with him he suspected she'd gotten scared because she hadn't had a free moment since they'd slept together. He thought her actions were deliberate.

Plotting with her secretary had been his only option.

He knew she was going to keep making him work to get back into her good graces. She might not be doing it intentionally, but she was definitely avoiding him. And he'd had enough of that.

Having her here in his bedroom felt right. It was the place he thought of when he pictured her with him.

He put her tote on the padded bench at the end of the bed. "Would you like a bath?"

"Yes. I think I would."

"I'll draw you one while you open this," he said, handing her a gift-wrapped box.

He left before she opened it. The ultramodern bathroom was an oddity for the UK, but he'd seen it in a magazine and decided he wanted one. It was large, with a garden tub and a stained-glass window that overlooked the backyard. He had a glass-enclosed double shower and a steam room in the space as well. The double sinks had a marble countertop.

He drew the bath for Ainsley and added some soothing bath salts he'd had his secretary order. He turned on the heated towel racks and checked to see that the champagne he'd left chilling was still cold. He popped the cork and poured them both a glass.

When he went back into the bedroom, she was still sitting on the padded seat with the gift box on her lap.

"You didn't open it."

"I was waiting for you," she said.

"I'm here," he said.

She toyed with the white ribbon on the box. "Why did you get me a gift?"

"Not so we could play twenty questions. Are you going to open it or not?"

She ripped the paper, folded it into a neat square and put it next to her on the bench. Then she opened the shirt-sized box. She drew back the tissue paper and pulled out the La Perla negligee. She pulled it from the box and held it up in front of her.

"Thank you."

"You're welcome. I wanted to find something that was as sexy as you are, but this was as close as I could come."

She blushed. "I'm not sexy."

"Then my memories of our night together must be wrong. Because I remember a very sexy woman in heels, hose and a garter belt seducing the hell out of me. Ready for your bath?" he asked, raising one eyebrow.

"Yes." Ainsley kicked off her shoes and then stood up to follow him into the bathroom. A sigh escaped her when her bare feet hit the heated wooden floor. This bathroom—this entire house—had been designed with comfort and luxury in mind.

He turned off the taps of the tub, helped her take off her clothes and then hugged her close. "I missed you."

"Me, too," she said. The weeks apart had been long and made her realize how important Steven was to her.

He undressed and they both got in the tub, sitting behind her and drawing her into his arms and back against his chest.

She sighed again as she relaxed against him. He cupped her breasts in his hands as she let her head rest against his shoulder. Her head tipped to look up at him.

"Tell me what you've been so busy with that you couldn't see me," he said.

"Work. Seriously, that's all I've been doing. I have to go to parties and dinners and every minute of my day is claimed by someone."

"I want to be that someone. I thought you wanted a

relationship," he said. He circled his fingers around her areola.

She shifted her shoulders and the tips of her pink nipples poked up through the suds in the tub. From his perspective, her body was all creamy skin, white soap bubbles and then there were those pink nipples...

"I do want one. I just didn't anticipate both of us being so busy. What have you been doing?"

"Getting the North American unit up to speed."

"How did you do that?"

"I sent my best man to do the job—Dinah. She works for me at Raleighvale."

"Is it hard running two companies?" she asked.

"Not for me," he said.

He lifted one hand from her breast and tipped her chin up. He leaned down and kissed her long and deep. Just what he'd wanted to do ever since she'd walked out of Heathrow.

She turned in his arms until she straddled him. He hadn't had a chance to have her on top of him as they made love, and he wanted to be able to see her face above his as he took her.

He cupped the water from the tub and rinsed her breasts off. Her nipples beaded in the air as his hands left them, replacing his touch with his mouth. She pushed her fingers into his thick dark hair and drew him to her.

Steven knew he'd revealed too much of himself by bringing her here, but as she shifted on him, her warmth replacing the warmth of the water in the tub, he didn't care.

He wanted this woman. He knew he couldn't take her in the tub. He needed to put on a condom before that happened, but for now it was enough to tempt both of them.

To let the tip of him tease the entrance of her body as his mouth moved over her breasts.

She wrapped her arms around him and hugged him close to her. He needed to keep her by his side, he thought. Marriage?

"Make love to me, Steven."

"Yes," he said, standing to lift her out of the tub and carry her into his bedroom. Thoughts of marriage would wait until later.

Twelve

Steven wrapped Ainsley in one of his big bath towels and carried her to his bed. He took a minute to dry off and then reached for the box of condoms he had in the nightstand drawer. He removed one and sheathed himself before falling down next to her on the bed.

"I thought you'd want to see me in that beautiful nightgown," she said.

"Not until I've had a proper welcome home. Then you can try on whatever you want."

She laughed. "I missed this."

"Did you? Then why did you refuse my calls while you were in Milan?"

He shifted on the bed so he was lying on top of her. He braced his elbows on either side of her body to keep most of his weight from her, but probed the entrance to her body.

She twined her arms around his neck, lifted herself up

and kissed him. "I wanted to make sure that you really wanted me. And I knew if you were serious about me, then you'd still want me when I returned to London. After you left that morning, I needed to know that I was as important to you as you are to me."

"I'll show you how important you are," he said sliding into her body inch by inch, taking his time and claiming her.

"I hope you can," she said softly. She wanted to believe in Steven, yet knew she still didn't trust him with her heart.

She held tightly to his shoulders as he began to thrust into her. She stopped talking and her eyes closed as her head fell back. He wanted to draw out their lovemaking, but couldn't. It had been too long since he'd had her and he felt his orgasm coming fast.

He tried to hold back, wouldn't come before she did. He whispered hot, sexy words into her ear. Brought his hand up between their bodies and caressed her breasts, teasing her nipples until he heard her gasp and then the sound of her low moan as she climaxed.

"Come for me," he said.

He held himself still as her body pulsed around him and then he started thrusting again. He ducked his head, caught her nipple between his lips and sucked on her until he felt his orgasm explode though him. He was blinded by it as he thrust into her two, then three times, until he was completely drained.

He collapsed next to her on the bed, using a corner of her towel to wipe the moisture from between her legs. He went to wash off and then came back to bed, pulling her into his arms.

"Now that pressing matters are out of the way, what were you saying? You were testing me?"

She pinched his side. "Yes, I was. I don't want to be the only one who has something at stake here."

"And what makes you think that you are?"

"Because you left," she said. "If you'd stayed that morning…well, I would have felt more confident."

"Why don't you?" he asked. She was lying on his chest and toying with the light hair that covered him. Her lowered head hid her expression.

"You're the first man I've felt this way about," she said. "And you aren't like my magazine. I can't manage you the same way."

"Why can't you?"

She shrugged. "Because I care about you, Steven. I've really missed you."

He hugged her tight for a minute. He was glad to hear that she cared about him. It meant a hell of a lot more than he'd thought it would.

"If you hadn't been playing games, we could have enjoyed the last three weeks."

She pushed herself up on an elbow and looked down at him. "I wasn't the only one."

"No, you weren't," he admitted. At first he'd been waiting for her to make the first move. After all, she was the one who'd wanted a relationship. But it hadn't taken him long to realize what she was doing. So now he was here with her in his arms and he didn't want to let her go. He was going to ask her to be his wife.

That was dangerous thinking for a man with no roots. A man who always moved on. He wasn't looking for a permanent home. He reached over and turned off the light. He didn't want to dwell on that now.

She curled on her side and fell asleep but he stayed

awake, holding her as tightly as he wanted to because there was no one but the moon and stars to see him.

In the quiet of the night, he realized his half-hatched plan of an engagement wasn't going to work. Ainsley cared about him. She was going to want the whole shebang. She wasn't going to settle for some long-term engagement just so he could sleep with her every night.

He only knew that he wanted her by his side and he was going to have to figure out how to make that happen. He wondered if she'd stop playing games now that he'd made the first move.

He hoped so, because he wasn't going to let her retreat back into her shell. He wasn't going to let her use work as an excuse to keep him at arm's length. He was in charge of this relationship and he would set the terms.

The words were strong and he knew he could say that now in the middle of the night, but in the cold light of day... he would do whatever it took to ensure that she was in his arms every night.

She stirred in her sleep as he squeezed her tight—too tight. He soothed her and then tried to go to sleep, but he held her for a long time before drifting off. He kept watching her face. He had to figure out how to keep her from meaning too much.

Ainsley woke up alone in Steven's big bed. There was a note on the nightstand. She reached over and picked it up. She'd forgotten to remove her contacts last night so she had no problem reading it.

Steven's spidery scrawl read:

I'm in my home office on a conference call. New toothbrushes in the medicine chest. Breakfast on the deck at 10.

She climbed out of bed, surprised by her own nudity. But as she stood there in the room, she found that she wasn't uncomfortable. Steven loved her body and she was coming to like it, too. She was coming to realize that she was the woman she saw in the mirror. That wasn't a facade but who she really was.

When she got downstairs, he was still on the phone and gestured for her to wait on the deck. She brought her BlackBerry with her and checked her e-mail. Freddie had sent her one saying that Maurice, the publisher of their magazine, needed to talk to her urgently.

She dialed his number in New York and was put through immediately to his office.

"It's Ainsley," she said when he came on the line.

"Good. Did you get Malcolm Devonshire?"

"Not yet. I'm still working on it. I did get all three of the mothers."

"That's great. As I mentioned before, I'm going to use your articles here in the States, as well. The Everest Group is going to relaunch the Manhattan Mega Store through an in-store event with XSU, the new group that's just signed with Everest Records. It will be their North American CD launch."

"Great. I assigned Bert Michaels to do the interviews with the mums. I think I might have to assign someone to do a sidebar piece on XSU. That's a nice plus.

"Also, I wanted to make sure you know that Steven Devonshire and I are dating. Are you still okay with that?" she asked Maurice.

"I am. I think as long as you're circumspect and we keep the focus off Steven, we'll be fine."

"Okay. I'll have to talk to my assistant about which

writer we have available to do the XSU interview. Let me call you right back."

"Just send it via e-mail. I want to know about Malcolm by close of business tomorrow."

"No problem," she said. But she had absolutely no idea how she was going to make that happen. Malcolm wouldn't even return her calls. She knew he also had an estate in Surrey. She'd have to get Steven to take her there today—it couldn't be that far. The sooner she talked to him the better.

She called her office and gave Cathy a list of things to do today. She hung up just as she heard Steven behind her. He walked out with a tray of fruit salad and juice.

"I had my housekeeper prepare this for us. Do you want something heavier for breakfast?"

"No. This is perfect," she said. She hated eating breakfast. That was probably part of the reason she tended to overeat all day. So she'd started eating something small. But she still didn't really like breakfast.

"Do you have anything planned for us today?" she asked.

"Is there something you'd like to do?" he asked.

"Yes. I'd like to meet your biological father."

Steven shook his head. "Afraid you're on your own there."

"Why? Steven, this is important to me. My boss is going to run the interviews with your mothers in our U.S. magazine as well. This is huge. If I get Malcolm to agree—"

"Sorry, Ainsley. I don't talk to him. You can call his attorney and see if you can work something out."

She shook her head. "Did you two have a falling out?"

"I don't want to talk about this."

She stood up and walked over to him. "I do. This is important to both of us."

He shook his head. "Not to me. I don't need Malcolm Devonshire."

"Then why are you working for him?"

"So I can show him up."

She realized that she was making him angry. She didn't understand why he couldn't simply call his father…except that he always referred to Malcolm as Malcolm, not Dad.

"Do you want to talk about it?"

"Why? So you can get some juicy tidbits to add to your article? Or because you care for me?"

"I do care about you."

"Then let this go," he said.

"I can't. It might be the writer in me but I want to know more."

"What does that matter to you? Isn't it enough to talk to my mother and Malcolm's other sons about our business?"

She crossed her arms under her breasts and watched him. "This isn't about the article anymore. This is about you and me. I want to know why you're so upset."

He turned away from her. Placing the tray on the table, he stalked over to the railing. His house overlooked a beautiful plot of land, and she felt as if the rest of the world didn't exist.

But it did. There were bosses to answer to and articles to get published. She knew she should just let him be, but she couldn't.

She walked over to him, putting her hand on his back. "I'm sorry, Steven."

"For what?" he asked, glancing down at her.

"For not realizing that Malcolm was just a sperm donor and not a father to you."

He turned to face her and she wondered if she'd misjudged him. Had she said the wrong thing?

"Sperm donor? That's brilliant. I've never heard him described that way before, but you certainly pegged it."

"You may have noticed that I'm pretty good at observing people and figuring out what makes them tick." She smiled, half in relief.

"I am, too, which is why I'm so good as a CEO," he said.

"You are good as a man, too," she said.

"You might be the only one who thinks so."

She doubted that. Steven didn't let people in. She wasn't sure that she was the only one who cared for him. As she watched him look out over his property, pretending his parentage didn't matter, she suddenly realized that she loved him.

Steven knew that he'd made a mistake by bringing Ainsley here. Now that she was here, he wanted to get her back to the city. Anywhere he could put barriers between them. It was fine if they were going to have a relationship. That was something he could definitely handle. But if she was going to keep asking questions about Malcolm outside of the articles she was having written…well, then she had to go.

He never thought about the lack of a father in his life. Men like Roman had long filled the gap as father figures when he'd been a young boy. But once he'd gone off to Eton he'd been on his own. There had been men that he'd learned things from when he'd been starting out in business, but for the most part he was a loner.

That's right, he reminded himself. He was a loner. He didn't have room in his life for a woman with soft violet eyes and compassionate hugs.

The only thing he needed a woman for was sex. He and Ainsley were white-hot in bed, but that didn't mean he wanted to open his veins and bleed for her in private. The article was his public face and no one saw the private man—not even Ainsley.

"You haven't said anything in almost thirty minutes," she said.

"You haven't, either," he said. They were eating lunch on the patio at his house. He'd shown her his estate and the quiet day he'd envisioned for them hadn't turned out as he'd planned. They were both tiptoeing around each other and he knew it was past time to get back to the city and back to work.

"I was afraid of saying the wrong thing again."

"You won't," he said. Because he'd buttoned up his emotions and tucked them away. He wouldn't react as he had earlier. He just hadn't expected her to ask him questions outside of the article. If you asked most people about seeing their father, it wouldn't be a big deal. But he was a Devonshire bastard and even if Ainsley wanted to put a better spin on it, the world knew that Malcolm wasn't much of a father to the boys he'd sired.

But he'd spent his life knowing that his father hadn't wanted to have anything to do with him. That was why he'd been so reluctant to go to that meeting at the Everest Group and, conversely, why he was so determined to win the contest Malcolm had set in motion. He wanted to show the old man that he—Steven—was better at the business Malcolm had dedicated his life to.

He checked his e-mail on his iPhone and saw that

Dinah was back from the States. She'd sent a long file of recommendations and that was just what he needed—to bury himself in work at the office. He felt a twinge of regret that he wasn't going to follow through on his plan to ask her to live with him, but their awkward conversation today had reminded him what living with someone would entail.

When you were dating you didn't have to share every detail of your life, but once you moved in… Then came resentment and anger and he didn't need that. Steven Devonshire was a rock—an island—and he needed nothing.

"I have to get back to the office. A bit of an emergency has come up."

She nodded. "Let me get my bag and I'll be ready to go."

She went back into his house and he watched her go. Knew she'd never be here again. A part of him was really going to miss her. He liked Ainsley more than anyone he'd slept with in a long time. Hell, forever. He'd never met a woman who got to him the way she did.

And she would never know. *Could* never know, because if she did then she'd want things from him that he'd never be able to give her.

She came back down with her bag and he went to get the car, realizing that he'd simply been sitting there waiting for her the entire time. She did that to him—made him forget the parts of himself that he'd always taken for granted and now he wanted to be that man again. He was a man who didn't care and was always looking ahead. He would get back to being that way again, he vowed.

He pulled the car up to the front of the house and went in to get her. She was standing in the foyer, thanking his housekeeper for the breakfast she had made.

"Thank you for bringing me here," she said to him.

"No problem. Sorry we can't stay longer," he said.

"No, you aren't. You've been trying to get me out of here ever since I asked about Malcolm."

He shouldn't have been surprised that she saw right through him, but he was taken aback that she'd said anything. She had let him take the lead, let him be the one to make the bold moves, and now suddenly she was taking charge.

"I have been. I realized that I'd let a journalist into my house—into my sanctuary. I know I suggested the articles, but I invited you here for personal reasons."

"I wasn't in here snooping around and trying to find out your secrets. You and I are lovers, and I asked you for a favor. If I'd realized what your relationship with Malcolm was, I never would have asked," she said.

"What is my relationship with him?"

"Nonexistent. Right?"

"Very true," he said, opening the car door for her. "Get in."

"I'm not done talking yet," she said.

"I am."

He held the door a minute longer and she just stood there with a sullen look on her face. A part of him knew he was being unfair to her, but she was asking questions and pointing out things that he never wanted to talk about.

"I'm leaving. Are you going with me or not?"

"Of course I'm going with you. I can't believe you are letting this get so out of control."

"It's not me," he said. "It's you and your magazine article. Prying into lives of people who don't want to be pried into."

"*You* are the one who wanted some compensation for letting us shoot in your store."

"That's right, I did. Just the heirs and our businesses. You had to drag family into it. Never thinking that Malcolm Devonshire only ever had one family and it was a corporate business unit."

"I'm so sorry to hear that because then he missed out on three incredible sons," she said. She brushed past him and climbed into the car.

Thirteen

After driving the entire way in silence, Steven dropped her off at her office and then drove away. She knew that she'd pushed too hard with him. But that hadn't been her intent. She had no idea why things had gone south so quickly. There was one thing she knew and it was her job. When she was in her office, she was in control. It was the one place where she didn't have to answer to anyone but herself.

Cathy was surprised to see her when she walked in. "I thought you were taking the day off."

"I changed my mind. Maurice wants us to lock up the interview with Malcolm. I need you to find out who his attorney is and get me an appointment with him. Did you get the schedule of when we need answers for the article?"

"I did. I'm glad you're here. I was just getting ready to call you. We had a minor emergency with the photo shoot for next month's cover. The model we're using is refusing to wear the outfit the creative director picked out."

"This is the shoot we're doing here in the building, right?"

"Yes. But she's in your office with the creative director."

Ainsley pushed open her office door and saw the creative director, the model and the photographer all sitting there. "What's going on?"

"He vants me to wear this," the model said, standing up and gesturing to her outfit.

"Do I know you?"

"No."

"Then sit down. Tell me why I'm wasting money on another photo shoot," she said.

"She just did a shoot for *Cosmo* and wore an outfit similar to this."

"Really?" she asked the girl. "What's your name?"

"Paulina."

"We're trying to find something different for her to wear," the creative director said. "But everything I've pulled together isn't working. I know you were in Milan…"

"Go back to the fashion closet and find something different. Here are the sketches I brought back from Milan. Let's find something inspired by these. It's different."

"Agreed. Thanks, Ains. You're a lifesaver."

"And my head is on the chopping block if I screw up this magazine," she muttered to herself after they left.

She walked over to her desk, but didn't sit down. Instead she went into her private bathroom and washed her face. She didn't look at herself in the mirror because she didn't want to see the stranger looking back at her. Not again.

Before Steven, she had felt as if she were wearing a

costume when she looked in the mirror—that the slim and pretty woman she saw wasn't really her. But now she knew that she had started to accept who she was and if she looked in the mirror again she was going to see a woman who'd made a huge mistake.

A woman who'd trusted the wrong man and let herself get hurt. From the beginning she'd known that Steven held a part of himself back from anyone he got involved with. She might have mistaken his reactions for those of a man who was uncomfortable letting others see him. But the truth was she suspected that he didn't feel anything at all, that he played at having emotions.

Just as he'd said to her that he couldn't love. And she'd foolishly thought that he was just saying that. That he didn't want her to build castles around him, and make him into something he wasn't.

That wasn't fair, she thought. She had no idea what kind of man he was; she kept expecting him to be one way and was surprised when he wasn't. The truth was she'd allowed herself to be angry with him because she'd realized she'd overstepped her bounds.

She had taken his idea for an article about the business and the men of the Everest Group and turned it into an article about the women in Malcolm Devonshire's life, which was what it had to be for *FQ*. Had she simply been looking for a salacious angle she could use to sell magazines?

It was only now that she'd fallen in love with him that she wanted the details for herself. Not for the magazine or the world, but for her. She wanted to know what it was like for him to grow up in the shadows.

She didn't have to ask how it had affected him because she saw how guarded he was with her—with everyone. He worked all the time and was driven to prove to the world that he didn't need anyone. She knew he'd deny it, but that was what Steven Devonshire was doing.

She wondered what he'd meant by the competition and wanting to beat his brothers. She knew that Steven had left his retreat with her because she'd made him uncomfortable. How could she make amends for that? And how could he? She'd reached out to him not to hurt but to help him.

She was still thinking about that when the phone rang. "This is Ainsley."

"Hello. This is Henry Devonshire. I'm having a get-together at this weekend's London Irish Rugby game and wanted to invite you. My half brothers will be there and my mum as well. You'd have a chance to see what my life is like away from the record label."

"I'd like that, Henry. May I bring Bert Michaels along? He's the writer doing the interview."

"Yes. That's fine. I'll leave tickets at the Will Call window."

"Thanks."

She was still going to see Steven whether they were involved or not. And she didn't know how she was going to handle that.

Being professional was one thing, but seeing the man she loved and having him ignore her… She needed to talk to him before the rugby match. She needed to figure out if she'd damaged irreparably what they had. There was only one way for her to do that. She had to call him or go to his office.

She sent him an e-mail to see if he was going to respond or ignore her.

Thank you for a lovely evening. Please join me for dinner tonight.

She didn't have to wait long. A few minutes later she had a response from him.

Are you asking as a magazine editor or my lover?

She hit Reply and knew if she had to choose between the articles she was publishing and Steven, she'd pick him.

Lover.

His response came back a minute later.

Then yes. I'm done at eight. I'll pick you up.

She thought about it for a moment and realized that she wanted to do something nice for him. Something like what he'd done for her last night.

Meet me at my house. I'll have dinner for us.

She left the office early and stopped at Tesco's on her way home to pick up the ingredients for a light pasta sauce and garlic bread. She wasn't much of a cook and if his aunt was a chef, he wasn't going to be impressed by anything she made. But staying in seemed like a good idea tonight. She wanted to be alone with Steven.

She needed the chance to repair the damage she'd done when she'd let her desire to get ahead get in the way of her relationship with Steven. And she didn't want anything to come before the man she loved.

Steven had to park down the block from Ainsley's house when he got there. He had a bottle of wine in one hand and a copy of Steph Cordo's new CD in the other. He knew he'd been a bit of a bear when she'd brought up Malcolm. But he couldn't help it.

He didn't talk about his family—ever. But he'd talked about his mum and Malcolm with Ainsley and that made him wonder if he should have turned down her dinner invite. But he couldn't. He wanted to see her again.

It didn't matter that she made it hard for him to focus on work. He was drawn to her like a moth to a flame and no matter that he knew it would end the same way the moth's life did, he was still plunging ahead.

He rapped on her door and waited in the damp April evening for her to answer. She opened the door a few minutes later. She wore a Betsey Johnson apron and had bare feet. She hadn't changed out of the same jeans and T-shirt that she'd had on when they'd left his place in Surrey.

And she looked eminently kissable.

He took her in his arms as soon as he stepped over the threshold. Pulled her close and kissed her for all he was worth. He used his mouth and his lips to tell her that he was sorry for the way he'd overreacted.

When he set her on her feet, she stepped back away from him. She put her fingers on her lips and looked up at him. He saw there were tears in her eyes.

"Don't cry."

"It's just… I'm sorry I asked those questions. I was doing it because I care about you, not to get a scoop for our writers to use," she said.

"It's okay. You just found my one hot button."

She tipped her head to the side. "Do you only have one?"

He thought about it. Malcolm was the only topic that always set him off. Even as a child he'd been quick to get into fights with other kids at school when they brought up Malcolm or his bastard brothers.

"Yes, just one sets off my temper."

"But you have other hot buttons?" she asked, leading the way into her kitchen. The scent of garlic and tomatoes filled the air and he almost moaned. The combo was one he loved. She gestured for him to have a seat at the small table in the kitchen.

"I have hot buttons for sex," he said. "Do you have a corkscrew? I'll open the wine and pour us each a glass."

"I do. How can you casually mention sex and wine in the same sentence?"

"Easily," he said. "When I'm around you, sex is always on my mind."

"Is that the only reason we're together?" she asked.

He found the corkscrew and opened the bottle of merlot she had sitting by two glasses on the table. "Sex?"

"Yes," she said, "I'd like to think there is more to us than sex."

"There is," he assured her. But he didn't know what it was and he hoped she wouldn't ask him. "Do you need my help cooking?"

"Maybe. I'm not a master chef. But I think I've got the pasta and sauce. If you want to check the garlic bread that would be great."

He did and they had a nice dinner talking about nothing important. He sensed that she was on edge. It was the first time she had been that way around him since they'd become lovers.

"What's made you so nervous?" he asked her after they cleaned up the dinner dishes.

"I just realized today that you mean more to me than I

thought you did and I don't want to say anything to make you leave."

There was more vulnerability in that sentence than he'd expected and he had no idea how to respond. Her candor startled him.

"Don't build too many dreams on me, love. I'm still just one of the Devonshire bastards. A man who was born one has a hard time leaving that behind."

"You aren't a bastard with me, Steven. And I can't help having dreams of the two of us together. Even when we were apart, I thought about you."

Steven leaned back in his chair and took a long sip of his wine. He didn't want to let her know he'd missed her. She already had too much power over him. Right now he was hard just listening to her talk about the kinds of wine she liked. How much ammo should he give her?

"I'm glad to hear that. Why did you make me wait so long before you asked to see me again?"

She shrugged. The vulnerability in her eyes returned and it made his heart miss a beat. He didn't want to see her looking like that. He wanted her happy and confident.

"Tell me," he urged her when it seemed she wasn't going to say anything.

"I was afraid."

"Of what?"

"Well, I've been obsessed with you since I wrote that article five years ago. And I wasn't sure if this new thing between us was just me wanting someone I couldn't have. I mean, five years ago I was fat."

"Five years ago I was blind. Because I like you, Ainsley," he said, even though he'd had no intention of saying anything. "Your body is sexy, but it's who you are that attracts me."

She blinked, got up and walked away from the table. He followed her to find she was crying.

"What did I say?"

"Just exactly the right thing," she said, turning and throwing herself in his arms. "I love you, Steven."

He froze, his arms halfway around her. *Love*. Damn. Normally he was adept at avoiding these kinds of relationship talks, but Ainsley had knocked him off track earlier with her questions about Malcolm and tonight with her apology. And he was gobsmacked.

She was staring up at him. Her wide violet eyes beaded with her tears and he knew he had to say something. But had no idea what to say.

He cared for her; he wanted her. But love? He had no idea what that even felt like and he had no idea how he was going to find the right words for this moment.

"Thank you."

"Thank you?" Ainsley hadn't spent a lot of time thinking about what kind of response Steven would give to her profession of love, but she'd expected something more than *thank you*.

"Yes. But I'm not sure what you see that you think is worth loving," he said.

In that moment she realized that the sexy, charming man was damaged. Why hadn't she realized it earlier? His parents' abandonment had left him as vulnerable as her weight had left her.

When he looked in the mirror, he saw someone who couldn't love and when she looked in the mirror, she saw someone who was fat.

"It's okay. I see the real you," she said.

"What do you see, Ainsley?" he asked her.

She struggled to put into words what she felt for him. It was ephemeral. More emotions than tangible qualities. But she knew what he wanted. Because he'd shown her that she was sexy despite her fears.

"I see a man who is very caring and careful with me and my emotions."

He shook his head. "You see a man who wanted to get you into bed and did everything in his power to make that happen."

She looked at him and felt the first hint of doubt that Steven was the man she thought he was.

"I see a man who took time out of his busy schedule to give me a day off and to make time for us."

Again he gave her that hard look of his. One that she was coming to seriously dislike. "I needed to work from home that day. It worked out for me."

She walked away from him and then turned back to face him. "What is your problem? Why can't you see what I do?"

"I have no idea. Maybe you wanted to see something in me that wasn't there. Some kind of fantasy based on that interview you did five years ago. I'm not that man."

She pointed her finger at him. "You could be, you just don't want to. Because you're a coward."

"I've hit men for saying that."

"You're not going to hit me and we both know it."

"That's right, but I will walk out this door."

"If you do, then it will be because you're afraid. Afraid to take a chance on something good and lasting."

He walked to her and for the first time she wished she'd left her shoes on because she could use a couple of extra inches right now. She felt overweight and weak compared to him. But she knew she wasn't.

Her size had never truly defined her. She might have let it at one point, but she was smart, funny and sexy no matter what her weight was. And right now she knew that she was worth loving. She always had been. This man was going to realize at some point that he'd given up on something good.

"Love like this doesn't come along every day, Steven. And if you walk out my door, you will miss me. Tonight, tomorrow and a hundred other tomorrows, because you will end up alone."

"Thanks for the prediction, Madame Ainsley, but I don't need your second sight to tell me that. I like to be alone. You and me, we had some hot sex and that was it."

She shook her head. "You can't even see what you are throwing away." She couldn't stop the tears that burned, but she refused to let them fall. Blinked and blinked until they pooled at the bottom of her eyes.

"Don't do that. Don't look at me with those wide, wet violet eyes and try to make me feel guilty," he said.

"I'm not trying to make you feel anything. I wanted to love you, but you're too set in your own ways to understand that love isn't a trap."

He gave her a cynical look that made her shiver. "Sorry, love, but I know better. I've seen my mother trapped by her feelings for her work. And my father couldn't even leave his true love—the Everest Group—to *meet* his sons, much less spend time with them.

"I know what love is but it's not the same love that you're talking about."

She wrapped one arm around her waist and watched him. There were no words to make this okay. Not for him and certainly not for her. She knew when he had a chance to think…hell, what did she really know about him?

But she didn't know if he'd come to the realization that she was worth keeping before she moved on. Before she looked at him and was filled with apathy, not empathy.

"I think you should go," she said.

"I think so," he said, picking up his suit jacket and walking toward the door. "For what it's worth, I'm sorry. I did enjoy every minute we spent together. You are a very special lady, Ainsley."

Then he walked out the door and she stood there watching him go, watching him walk down her block away from her. A light rain fell and he didn't quicken his pace, just kept moving steadily, inexorably toward his car.

She closed the door and wrapped both arms around her waist, feeling as if she were falling apart. She had no idea how she was going to recover from this. She hadn't thought she could feel this bad from a person again. No one had ever hurt her like him. He'd hurt her badly five years ago, and she didn't want to admit he'd done it again.

She sat there for a long time, tears burning at the back of her eyes. Finally, she just drew her knees up to her chest and put her head down. She let her tears fall freely, knowing that they were going to come one way or another.

Her cell phone rang and she thought about getting up to answer it. It might have been Steven, but she knew it wasn't him. He would have come back if he'd had a change of heart.

And she would have let him in. Even though he'd said those things, she still loved him and she had a feeling she would for a long time.

Fourteen

Steven knew he'd made a mistake the first time he'd slept with Ainsley. She was a mass of contradictions and she made him care too much.

The rest of the week passed in a haze. Dinah had gone above and beyond on her recommendations for the North American operation with detailed notes for all the locations. She was turning that line of business around. He wouldn't have anything to base that on, other than his gut instinct, until the first financials came in at the end of the month, but so far each day they were improving and were way above last year's revenue at this same time.

His business unit was outperforming Henry's by a hair and Geoff was struggling, thanks to rising gas prices. But now, he didn't care about winning the competition with his half brothers anymore. All he really wanted was... Ainsley.

But he'd made damn sure that she was out of his life. He hoped she moved on quickly, but he knew the way he'd ended things would take time for her to recover from.

But as she'd sweetly listed all the reasons why she loved him, he had felt so afraid. Not for her, because she so obviously loved him, but for himself, because he felt the same way. He wanted desperately to spend the rest of his life with her.

With one person.

And that was a weakness he'd never allowed himself before this. Never even encountered. So he'd done the one thing he could think of: end things. End them in a way that would leave him no way to go back to her. Because if he'd left even a hint of an open door there, he knew he'd come back and break that door down.

And if he held her in his arms again, he was keeping her. He wasn't about to let her go. Not his Ainsley with her sweet smile and made-for-sin body, her brassy confident manner in the office and her shy sensuality in the bedroom.

He walked out of the bedroom at his apartment in London and into the living room to the bar. He pulled out a bottle of aged scotch and poured himself two fingers. He downed it and then poured himself another one.

There wasn't any amount of liquor that could drown this, however. No amount of thinking or rationalizing that was going to make the tears he saw in her eyes okay. He should never have been so brutal.

He knew from what she'd said that she'd been as lonely as he had been. And she'd tried to change her life first by losing weight and then by reaching out to him. By making love with him and then by loving him.

And he'd spurned her.

And for what?

He was a coward, just as she'd said. He was the worst kind of man. The same as his father, the man he'd never wanted anything to do with.

He picked up the phone despite the late hour and dialed her number. What was he going to say? He had no idea.

"Hello?"

Her sleepy voice made him smile and he knew he couldn't do it. He couldn't talk to her now when he was feeling like this. He needed to make sure he could be her man. And not run away the first time there was something he deemed too emotional.

He hung up without saying a word and sat back in the big leather chair of his. He found his cell and dialed Edmond's number.

The lawyer answered on the very first ring.

"This is Steven."

"Hello, Steven. What can I do for you?"

"Tell me why Malcolm even acknowledged my birth and the births of Henry and Geoff. It was clear he didn't want a family or heirs. So why did he?"

"I have no idea. At the time the Everest Group was struggling financially and he was trying very hard to get it back on track."

"Then why have heirs?"

"I think he wanted to ensure the company would live on after he died. I just don't think he knew how to focus on a woman and his business at the same time."

"Just like me."

"Indeed, sir. I've heard you are very like your father."

"In what way?" Steven asked.

"That you are a workaholic. Someone who focuses only on the bottom line."

"That doesn't make me like him. That makes me like

any other corporate shark," Steven said. "Ainsley called him a sperm donor and that's all he's been."

"I'm sorry that you feel that way. Malcolm did the best he could by you and the other heirs."

Steven thought about that for a very long time. "Have you ever—never mind. Sorry for bothering you so late."

"Not a problem, sir. Call me any time. Is there anything else?"

"Why haven't you called Ainsley back?" Steven asked.

"Malcolm doesn't talk to press."

"This isn't press. I have arranged a series of interviews with *Fashion Quarterly* magazine and I think the promo will be great for our company."

"Sounds good," Edmond said.

"It would be better with Malcolm. Will you ask him if he will answer a few questions?"

Edmond cleared his throat. "You know he—"

"Just ask him. Say it's the only thing that his son has ever asked of him."

"I will, sir."

Steven hung up—he was going to end up as Ainsley had painted him, but he hadn't realized that before this moment. He was going to end up alone with only his business partners at his deathbed.

And he didn't want that.

He wanted a different future. He wanted to have a wife and maybe a few kids with large violet eyes and pretty dark hair.

He wanted to have something to come home to and have Ainsley in his arms every night. And that was never going to happen unless he won her back.

And there was only one way to do that. He had to figure out how he could have her and not lose himself.

But after a lifetime of running away from attachments and emotions, he wasn't sure where to begin. He only knew that if he didn't he was going to end up like Malcolm Devonshire and he didn't want that.

He'd spent his entire life trying to prove to himself that he was better than his father and it was time he took the one risk that his biological father never had—love.

Ainsley didn't attend the rugby match, but sent her reporter instead with Freddie. They both had a wonderful time, which she gathered from Freddie's tweeting of the event. It got them some nice advance publicity for the articles that Bert was writing. He'd even wrapped up his piece on Henry. And she heard from him that he'd spoken to Steven and Geoff there as well.

The Devonshire heirs could be Freddie's show now. She didn't want to have to see any pictures of Steven; it was too hard. She woke up in the middle of the night missing his arms around her and that made her mad because before him she hadn't had anything to miss.

She'd spent her entire life alone, and had expected to continue it that way. But Steven had given her a glimpse—a hint—of what life could be, what it would be like to share her life with someone. And she wanted that.

She still craved his presence; she still needed him and loved him.

So when she got a DVD by special courier she wasn't sure what it was. It was marked "Devonshire Heirs," and when she opened it up and popped it into her DVD player she saw that it was a BBC One special interview with the Devonshire heirs. At first she was worried the interview would be similar to theirs, but luckily, the focus of the interview was different from the one she had Bert writing for their magazine. But the TV coverage certainly wouldn't detract from the articles they were running.

When the camera zoomed in on Steven, she was surprised to see how tired he looked. She took a few steps forward toward the screen, not even turning around when she heard her office door open.

"I think the main thing I've taken from my life was that I needed to be better than Malcolm. I wanted to make my own life—a better life. But I never realized that I was following the same path. Making the exact same mistakes," he said, looking directly into the camera.

She felt as if he were speaking directly to her.

"What mistakes have you made?" the interviewer asked.

There was a knock on her door and she paused the DVD.

"Yes?"

"It's quitting time and happy hour has come to you," Freddie said.

Cathy entered the room behind him with a pitcher of margaritas on a tray. "I'm not sure…"

"I am. This is your friend talking and you need a break."

"What are you watching?"

"An interview with the Devonshire heirs. Steven is about to talk about his mistakes."

Freddie put his arm over her shoulders without a word. He took the remote from her hand and pushed play.

"Being a workaholic and keeping everyone at arm's length. That made me successful in business, but it has left me rather isolated," Steven said.

"I'm sure there are women everywhere ready to help you fill your lonely nights."

Steven shrugged. "There's only one woman for me…if she'll still have me."

She couldn't believe what she heard. She stopped and replayed it. She watched it again and then pushed pause. "Is he talking about me?"

"I'm sure of it. You said he was going to come back to you some day," Freddie said. "It looks like that day came sooner than you thought."

"Do you think he's changed?"

Freddie lifted one shoulder. "Only you can decide."

"I'm so afraid. I still love him. How can I say no to a chance to have him in my life? It's what I've dreamed of."

"There's your answer," Freddie said.

"When did this air?" she asked. "How did I not hear about it?"

"It hasn't aired yet," Cathy said holding up the envelope it had come in. "There's a note from the producer saying that Steven asked for an advance copy to be sent to you."

"Is there a note from Steven in there?"

She shook the envelope and nothing came out. "Nope."

"What do I do?" she asked her two closest friends.

"I'd call him," Cathy said. "Whatever happened between you, it's obvious that he's sorry. His part of the interview was all about you."

She considered that but she'd made the last gesture, offered the last olive branch, and look how that had turned out. She wasn't sure she had the confidence to do it again. She just couldn't. She needed to see a sign from him.

What kind of sign?

"Freddie?"

"I'd wait, but then I'm not courageous when it comes to matters of the heart."

He wasn't and his track record was much longer than hers. Cathy and Freddie both looked at her as if they expected her to make a choice right then.

"I have to think about this. I'm scheduled to go to New York tomorrow. I'll call him when I get back. I can't jump back into that fire right now."

"Great idea. If he loves you, it doesn't come with an expiration date," Freddie said.

That's right. Was love forever? She hoped it would fade when it looked like she'd be heartbroken forever. But now? Should she jump in her MG and drive to find him? Though she missed him, she was going to have to wait until she was sure. Wait until the memory of the pain he'd inflicted on her subsided.

She worked until nine and went home to an empty house. She packed her carry-on bag and found the La Perla negligee that he'd given her still in the bag. She'd never had the chance to wear it for him. She held it up to herself and when it was time for bed she put it on.

She lay in her bed staring at the ceiling and thinking about Steven. She reached for her phone and almost called him but stopped herself. She wasn't ready.

A part of her wanted *him* to come back to *her* because he had been the one to walk away. She rolled on her side and hugged the pillow that he'd slept on to her stomach. It smelled faintly of him but the scent was fading and she knew she should probably go ahead and wash it, but she hadn't.

She'd just kept it here because she loved a man who was afraid to admit that he loved her. That interview intimated that he might have changed his mind, but she wasn't going to risk her heart on a maybe.

Steven had hoped she'd call him when she'd seen the interview, but she hadn't. He knew that he was going to have to show her that he loved her. That would take more than vague words on a taped interview. She needed and she deserved the big gesture.

He picked up his cell and called her friend Freddie.

"This is Steven Devonshire," he said when Freddie answered the phone.

"What can I do for you?" Freddie asked.

"I need your help to surprise Ainsley."

"Why? Do you just want her back in your bed or do you want her in your life for good?"

"I don't think that's any of your business," Steven said. He wasn't about to talk about his personal feelings with this guy.

"It is, because I had to pick up the pieces after you broke her heart—not once but twice. So you tell me that you aren't going to hurt her again or you can just hang up."

"I'm not going to hurt her again—you have my word."

"Okay, so what do you need from me?" Freddie said.

"I need Ainsley to come back to the Leicester Square store today at 2:00 p.m."

He hoped that Ainsley would be flattered that he remembered that the location was where they'd both met again. He wanted to go back to the beginning with her—not five years ago, but this time—and ask her to marry him.

"I'll do it. But why don't you just call her?"

"I want to surprise her," he said.

He hung up a few minutes later and realized that he was going to be very disappointed if Ainsley didn't show up. But he had a feeling she would. A woman like Ainsley didn't fall in love easily and he was counting on the fact that she did care deeply for him.

Ainsley finally spoke to Edmond, Malcolm's solicitor, and the man told her that Malcolm was too ill to be interviewed. Maurice was a little disappointed that they couldn't get Malcolm, but the articles on the mothers were so interesting that he was happy with that.

"I need to do photo shoots with the men and their mums. But otherwise I think this is wrapped up," she said to Maurice on the phone.

"I see you didn't mention a relationship with Steven in the draft of the article I received."

"We're…this is difficult, Maurice, but I'm not sure we have a relationship."

"Why not?"

"It's complicated."

"Everything in life is if you let it be. You found a way to get these articles done and kept from compromising your integrity. Why can't you figure out how to keep your relationship with him?"

"How do you know it's me?"

"I don't," Maurice said. "But you've been happier these last few weeks as we've secured the Devonshire women. I'd hate to see that end. Unless you were using him to get him to cooperate and then I might have to fire you."

"Maurice, I would never do that. I love him, but I'm not sure he loves me. I'm afraid—"

"That's all I needed to hear. I'm giving you to close of business today to resolve this issue."

"It's not an issue," she said to her boss. "It's my personal life and it's not as easy to sort out as a magazine."

"It's easier. You just have to trust your heart."

Maurice hung up and she wanted to scream. She was so afraid of letting Steven in, but she knew she had to do it; otherwise she would spend the rest of her life wondering what might have been.

Her phone rang.

"Ainsley Patterson."

"It's Freddie. Clear your calendar for this afternoon."

"Why?"

"It's a surprise."

"Freddie—"

"Don't bother asking because I'm not saying a word," he said.

"Fine. But I need to pick your brain about something."

"Okay, I'll be listening."

Steven had planned for every detail; now he just needed her to show up. His hands were sweating as he waited for her. Then suddenly she appeared. She walked into the store the way she had that first time. She wore a figure-flattering Betsey Johnson dress and walked toward him.

She stopped as she saw him. And Steven knew it was time for him to do his part. He walked forward and drew her into his arms, kissing her deeply. She tentatively held his shoulders. He held her close to him because it had been too long since he'd held her. And he needed her.

He pulled away and looked down into those wide violet eyes and he felt his heart clench.

"I'm so sorry, Ainsley. I was afraid and I never wanted to feel the same vulnerability that I saw in your eyes. I love you so much and I hope that you still love me."

He went down on one knee in front of her. "Please

say that you haven't given up on me and that you still love me."

Tears made her beautiful eyes watery and she stood there looking down at him.

"Seriously? After all the tears I've cried, I promised myself I wasn't going to cry over you again. But here I am."

"Love," he said, standing up. "I mean it. I'm not just spouting words. I love everything about you. Your curvy body, the way you smile at me in the morning. And I'm planning to spend the rest of our lives convincing you of that. I'd rather it be with you by my side but I'll keep trying to convince you no matter how long it takes," he said.

She took his hand, drew him to stand beside her, threw herself in his arms, wrapped her arms and legs around him and kissed him for all she was worth.

"I love you, Steven. I can't live without you. I'm so glad you came to your senses."

"Took me long enough," he said.

"It felt like a damn lifetime," she said.

"Will you marry me?" he asked.

"Yes, Steven, I will."

He slipped the ring on her finger and knew he'd finally found the home he'd always been searching for in this sexy woman's arms.

Epilogue

Ainsley and Steven spent the next few months living together and reassuring each other that they were meant to be together. When the articles ran in her magazine, she felt a sense of pride at the way the women came off. Malcolm Devonshire came off looking like a man who'd given up three successful women. And Ainsley felt sorry for Malcolm that he hadn't realized what he was missing.

The *Fashion Quarterly* articles on the Devonshire heirs and their mothers rocked the publishing world. Hearing the stories of the three women who'd given Malcolm Devonshire the publicity he'd needed to take the Everest Group to the next level had been publishing gold.

A few of the gossip Web sites had made a big deal of her relationship with Steven, but that had blown over and her boss, Maurice, didn't think it was anything to worry about.

"I can't believe you're getting married today," Freddie said.

"Me, either," she said.

Freddie came over and adjusted her veil. "I'm glad you finally found love."

She smiled at him. "I think it found me. What do you think?"

"Gorgeous, darling. I think that Maurice is going to regret not covering this event."

"I think he's done enough butting into my personal life," she said, remembering how her boss had pushed her to go after a life outside of work.

"Almost ready?"

"Yes. Is my dad?"

"He's outside and your mum is nervous. She said she never thought she'd see this day," Freddie said with a laugh.

She glanced out the window of the waiting room to where the wedding was taking place. The lovely rooftop garden overlooked Berne. It was decked out in flowers and twinkle lights.

"She's said the same thing to me several times," Ainsley said. "Is Steven here?"

"Of course he is," Freddie said. "I'm going out to reassure him now."

Freddie left and Ainsley sat back down on the padded bench. She'd never dreamed of a fairy-tale wedding but Steven wanted one. He wanted everything to be perfect for their special day and since his mother couldn't leave Berne and her work, they were getting married there.

He'd flown her parents to Switzerland and Freddie and

Cathy were going to be her attendants. His half brothers had attended and were standing up with him.

He'd changed from the man who was nothing but an island to a man who was surrounded by family and friends. They'd made their own family or at least the beginning of one. They were both workaholics and loved their jobs, so they'd decided not to have kids.

Neither of them had planned for children so it wasn't something they felt they'd missed. And Steven said loving her was something he was still trying to get comfortable with.

She had everything she'd never thought she'd have. When Lynn came out of the lab escorted by her fiancé, Roman, the wedding began. She'd met Lynn a few times and liked the woman. As well as her twin sister, Lucy. Both women loved Steven and though he'd always felt isolated, they'd always been there for him.

Her parents came in and hugged her.

"Your dress is exquisite," her mum said.

Ainsley had spent hours in Milan having the dress made. It was tight at the waist, low cut at the top, and fell in a straight line to the floor. There was a small train at the back of the dress.

She'd chosen a short, sassy-looking veil to wear over her glossy black hair.

"Thanks," Ainsley said. Her parents hugged her again and then went to sit down.

The wedding march started and instead of walking down the aisle with her father, she walked down by herself. Steven was waiting for her and kissed her as soon as she got to the altar. The minister went quickly through the vows and soon it was time for their first kiss as husband and wife.

It was long and sweet and everything that she had known it would be.

"I love you, Mrs. Devonshire."

"I love you, too, Mr. Devonshire."

* * * * *

Harlequin Intrigue top author
Delores Fossen presents a brand-new series of
breathtaking romantic suspense!
TEXAS MATERNITY: HOSTAGES
The first installment available May 2010:
THE BABY'S GUARDIAN

Shaw cursed and hooked his arm around Sabrina.

Despite the urgency that the deadly gunfire created, he tried to be careful with her, and he took the brunt of the fall when he pulled her to the ground. His shoulder hit hard, but he held on tight to his gun so that it wouldn't be jarred from his hand.

Shaw didn't stop there. He crawled over Sabrina, sheltering her pregnant belly with his body, and he came up ready to return fire.

This was obviously a situation he'd wanted to avoid at all cost. He didn't want his baby in the middle of a fight with these armed fugitives, but when they fired that shot, they'd left him no choice. Now, the trick was to get Sabrina safely out of there.

"Get down," someone on the SWAT team yelled from the roof of the adjacent building.

Shaw did. He dropped lower, covering Sabrina as best he could.

There was another shot, but this one came from a rifleman on the SWAT team. Shaw didn't look up, but he heard the sound of glass being blown apart.

The shots continued, all coming from his men, which meant it might be time to try to get Sabrina to better cover. Shaw glanced at the front of the building.

So that Sabrina's pregnant belly wouldn't be smashed

against the ground, Shaw eased off her and moved her to a sitting position so that her back was against the brick wall. They were close. Too close. And face-to-face.

He found himself staring right into those sea-green eyes.

How will Shaw get Sabrina out?
Follow the daring rescue and the heartbreaking
aftermath in THE BABY'S GUARDIAN
by Delores Fossen,
available May 2010 from Harlequin Intrigue.

HARLEQUIN *Presents*

Bestselling Harlequin Presents® author

Lynne Graham

introduces

VIRGIN ON HER WEDDING NIGHT

Valente Lorenzatto never forgave Caroline Hales's
abandonment of him at the altar. But now he's
made millions and claimed his aristocratic Venetian
birthright—and he's poised to get his revenge.
He'll ruin Caroline's family by buying out their
company and throwing them out of their mansion...
unless she agrees to give him the wedding night
she denied him five years ago....

**Available May 2010
from Harlequin Presents!**

Love Inspired

Former bad boy Sloan Hawkins is back in
Redemption, Oklahoma, to help keep his aunt's
cherished garden thriving and to reconnect with the
girl he left behind, Annie Markham. But when he
discovers his secret child—and that single mother
Annie never stopped loving him—he's determined
that a wedding will take place in the garden
nurtured by faith and love.

REDEMPTION RIVER

Where healing flows...

Look for

The Wedding Garden
by Linda Goodnight

*Available May 2010
wherever you buy books.*

www.SteepleHill.com

Steeple
Hill®

LI87595

® HARLEQUIN®

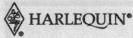
American ★ Romance®

LAURA MARIE ALTOM

The Baby Twins

Stephanie Olmstead has her hands full raising her twin baby girls on her own. When she runs into old friend Brady Flynn, she's shocked to find herself suddenly attracted to the handsome airline pilot! Will this flyboy be the perfect daddy— or will he crash and burn?

Babies & Bachelors USA

"LOVE, HOME & HAPPINESS"

www.eHarlequin.com

HAR75309

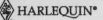

HARLEQUIN®

INTRIGUE®

**BESTSELLING
HARLEQUIN INTRIGUE® AUTHOR**

DELORES FOSSEN

**PRESENTS AN ALL-NEW
THRILLING TRILOGY**

TEXAS MATERNITY: HOSTAGES

When masked gunmen take over the maternity ward at a San Antonio hospital, local cops, FBI and the scared mothers can't figure out any possible motive. Before long, secrets are revealed, and a city that has been on edge since the siege began learns the truth behind the negotiations and must deal with the fallout.

LOOK FOR

THE BABY'S GUARDIAN, *May*
DEVASTATING DADDY, *June*
THE MOMMY MYSTERY, *July*

HI69472

REQUEST YOUR FREE BOOKS!

2 FREE NOVELS PLUS 2 FREE GIFTS!

Silhouette

Desire ®

Passionate, Powerful, Provocative!

YES! Please send me 2 FREE Silhouette Desire® novels and my 2 FREE gifts (gifts are worth about $10). After receiving them, if I don't wish to receive any more books, I can return the shipping statement marked "cancel." If I don't cancel, I will receive 6 brand-new novels every month and be billed just $4.05 per book in the U.S. or $4.74 per book in Canada. That's a saving of at least 15% off the cover price! It's quite a bargain! Shipping and handling is just 50¢ per book.* I understand that accepting the 2 free books and gifts places me under no obligation to buy anything. I can always return a shipment and cancel at any time. Even if I never buy another book, the two free books and gifts are mine to keep forever.

225/326 SDN E5QG

Name _____ (PLEASE PRINT)

Address _____ Apt. #

City _____ State/Prov. _____ Zip/Postal Code

Signature (if under 18, a parent or guardian must sign)

Mail to the Silhouette Reader Service:

IN U.S.A.: P.O. Box 1867, Buffalo, NY 14240-1867
IN CANADA: P.O. Box 609, Fort Erie, Ontario L2A 5X3

Not valid for current subscribers to Silhouette Desire books.

Want to try two free books from another line?
Call 1-800-873-8635 or visit www.morefreebooks.com.

* Terms and prices subject to change without notice. Prices do not include applicable taxes. N.Y. residents add applicable sales tax. Canadian residents will be charged applicable provincial taxes and GST. Offer not valid in Quebec. This offer is limited to one order per household. All orders subject to approval. Credit or debit balances in a customer's account(s) may be offset by any other outstanding balance owed by or to the customer. Please allow 4 to 6 weeks for delivery. Offer available while quantities last.

Your Privacy: Silhouette Books is committed to protecting your privacy. Our Privacy Policy is available online at www.eHarlequin.com or upon request from the Reader Service. From time to time we make our lists of customers available to reputable third parties who may have a product or service of interest to you. If you would prefer we not share your name and address, please check here. ☐

Help us get it right—We strive for accurate, respectful and relevant communications. To clarify or modify your communication preferences, visit us at www.ReaderService.com/consumerschoice.

SDES10R

HARLEQUIN® *Blaze*™

is proud to introduce...

New York Times bestselling author

Brenda Jackson

with

SPONTANEOUS

Kim Cannon and Duan Jeffries have a great thing going. Whenever they meet up, the passion between them is hot, intense...spontaneous. And things really heat up when Duan agrees to accompany her to her mother's wedding. Too bad there's something he's not telling her....

Don't miss the fireworks!

*Available in May 2010
wherever Harlequin Blaze books are sold.*

_____

red-hot reads

www.eHarlequin.com

HB79542